"Put me down, please, Colt...."

The calmness of Rowan's tone, the ease with which she spoke his name, lulled Colt into a complacent mood. Gently he lowered her to her feet and stood smiling, waiting for her directions.

Rowan moved so swiftly that Colt was taken completely off guard when she slipped into the bedroom, slammed the door shut, then turned the key with a loud decisive click.

"Rowan!" his voice boomed. She backed away in fear from the thud of fists on the heavy door, and from the anger evident even through a barrier of solid oak. "Don't be foolish. You can't run away forever from the responsibilities of marriage!"

"A marriage of convenience," she called back in a terrified treble. *"My convenience—not yours!"*

MARGARET ROME
is also the author of these
Harlequin Romances

and these
Harlequin Presents

Many of these titles are available at your local bookseller.

For a free catalogue listing all available Harlequin Romances and Harlequin Presents, send your name and address to:

HARLEQUIN READER SERVICE
1440 South Priest Drive, Tempe, AZ 85281
Canadian address: Stratford, Ontario N5A 6W2

Original hardcover edition published in 1981
by Mills & Boon Limited

ISBN 0-373-02487-8

Harlequin edition published July 1982

King of Kielder

by

MARGARET ROME

Harlequin Books

TORONTO • LONDON • LOS ANGELES • AMSTERDAM
SYDNEY • HAMBURG • PARIS • STOCKHOLM • ATHENS • TOKYO

CHAPTER ONE

WHEN she reached the Kielder Stone, a huge boulder through which ran the boundary line marking the division on the Border where England officially ceased and Scotland began, Rowan reined in her mount and sat motionless, staring down from a high vantage point over acres of forest land, an unbroken vista of conifer green that had remained undisturbed for decades—until recently.

Teeth bit sharply into a trembling bottom lip as she fought against a misery of tears. The battle had been staunchly fought, but victory had gone to the enemy, yet not even in solitude was she prepared to betray the proud traditions of a family that had survived generations of strife, bloodshed, and the bitter animosity of Scottish neighbours— thieving villains who had stolen across the border to steal sheep and cattle, to plunder the homes and even to kidnap the daughters of hated English Borderers.

Historians had attempted to prove that the blame had not been entirely one-sided, that there had been as many English reivers as there had been Scottish, and that during an era when the frontier territory had been dominated by dirk and sword—an arena where antagonists could meet— when blackmail, arson, robbery and murder had

5

been tolerated as normal, no householder of either nationality had dared to wander unarmed, to sleep without keeping one eye open, or to leave house, family or stock unguarded.

Over the years Rowan had conditioned her mind into accepting that not all Scots were black-hearted villains intent upon treachery, but recently she had been forcibly converted to her brother Nigel's vehemently expressed opinion that Border Scots were inculcated with a resentment of their English neighbours that was almost paranoic, that because of countless defeats both physical and political, they felt compelled to assuage a deep feeling of inferiority by launching devious, underhanded attacks upon a more affluent English society.

She winced when a harsh staccato noise rent the air, and bent to comfort the startled mare whose head had jerked in panic.

'Easy, Cello,' she murmured, stroking soothing hands along the length of a tautly arched neck, 'that was the sound of progress you heard, a sound we shall be forced to live with for the better part of a decade now that Colt Kielder and his associates have won their case. Industry is desperate for more water, you see,' numbly she intoned arguments that had been tossed back and forth between area authorities, conservationists and local residents during a tedious, months-long inquiry, 'also rising living standards have brought increased domestic demands in all parts of the region, which is why, because we happen to live in the most isolated and sparsely populated part of England, it has been decided that our quality of life is of little consequence, that families must be uprooted, roads and houses flooded, wildlife destroyed and animals made homeless in order to make way for a monster reservoir!'

As if mocking her agony, deriding the long bitter struggle she and her sympathisers had put up in an attempt to preserve the peace and tranquillity of the countryside they loved, a screeching cacophony of sound rose up from the valley where a huge tunnelling machine had begun an experimental probe to discover the type of rock strata likely to be encountered once the despoiling of nature was actually under way, and with an outraged sweep of powerful wings a rare peregrine falcon rose from a massive, untidy nest built of sticks, rubbish, rags and paper to demonstrate his displeasure by angrily beating the air.

Smothering a cry of regret, Rowan jerked upon the reins, wheeling Cello around so that she no longer had to face the noble falcon of war, the almost extinct airborne vision of grace that made the skies more beautiful. With hands loosely clasping the reins she allowed the mare to pick her own way down the fellside and slumped dejectedly in the saddle, her sadly brooding eyes lacking for the first time ever the sparkle of appreciation that usually ignited at the sight of a rippling lake overshadowed by darkly frowning fells, by windswept moorland and dense tracts of fir tree forest.

She was nearing home, cantering slowly along a main road slicing straight through the heart of dense woodland, when the sound of an approaching car jerked her shoulders erect, set her senses quivering. Nigel had often accused her of being 'fey', as acute as a witch in the art of premonition, and his notion was justified when she caught sight of a Land Rover being driven by the man whose presence her tense limbs and angry rise of colour had been quick to signal.

As if Cello, too, was sensitive to his awesome personality she trembled to a standstill when the Land Rover braked to a halt and its motor was cut, plunging them once more into a green-shrouded chasm of silence.

'Good morning, Lady Rowan!' Colt Kielder had the gall to smile as he eased his long, rangy frame out of the driving seat and strode towards her as if actually anticipating a welcome.

She was fiercely glad of having the advantage of being on horseback, so that for once she had no need to tilt her head in order to combat the challenge of steely grey eyes which, even in the midst of stormy dispute, had never been allowed to flicker with temper but had remained a cool, enigmatic contradiction to his shock of copper-red hair.

'That's a matter of opinion, Mr Kielder,' she managed to respond stiffly.

'Mister . . .?' She was incensed by the humourless quirk of his lips, by the relaxed, arrogant manner in which he seemed to take charge of every situation. 'As children, on the rare occasions when you and your brother were allowed to mix with village children, it was always impressed

upon me that you were to be addressed as Lady
Rowan and Lord Nigel respectively, but neither
of you appeared to have any reservations about
calling me Colt, so why the sudden formality? In
what way has the situation changed?'

'You dare to ask me that!' She shot bolt upright
in the saddle, her fingers itching to make contact
with the teak-tanned face leathered with hard
living that was hovering a tantalising slap-reach
away. Conscious that her inbred attitude of dignity was in danger of slipping, she stalled for time
by lifting a hand to push back from her brow a
wing of hair black as the plumage of the raven that
was doomed to be ousted from its natural habitat,
deprived of security and freedom at the instigation
of a man as insensitive and uncaring as his reiving
Scottish ancestors. Lashes swept dark as bruises
against flushed cheeks, her soft mouth trembled,
yet somehow she managed to keep her voice
steady when she husked:

'I think I could more easily have forgiven a
stranger for disrupting the privacy of our home,
for despoiling the beauty of our countryside with
bulldozers and earthdiggers, noisy lorries, and a
shanty town of workmen's caravans. But you were
one of us! Granted your family pulled up roots
and emigrated to America when you were twelve
years old, nevertheless, exactly like Nigel and
myself, you were *born* here!'

'*Exactly* like, Lady Rowan . . .?' His suspicion
of transatlantic accent became more pronounced,
nothing grating or abrasive enough to eliminate a
natural Scottish burr, more like the muted harsh-

ness of sound made when the gentle waters of a
burn tumble unexpectedly over a bed of gravel.
'I'm afraid the similarity escapes me, for while
you and your brother grew up in the rarified
atmosphere of Falstone Castle, cossetted from the
realities of life by a retinue of servants, my home
was a farmworker's cottage on your father's estate,
a tied house from which we were evicted because
my father had the temerity to speak out strongly
against some new method of farming that
offended him greatly. Yes, we emigrated,' he
nodded, 'but not from choice. It broke my father's
heart when he was forced to leave the countryside
he loved because no other employer in the area
would give work to a man who had been dismissed
from his previous job without a reference.'

'Oh . . .!' Her gasp throbbed with contrition.
'I'm so sorry, I had no idea . . .'

'Of course you hadn't,' he agreed with surprising magnanimity, 'you couldn't have been more
than six years old at the time. But even if you had
been old enough to understand, your inbred sense
of superiority would have prevented you from
finding fault with your father who, in common
with many landed gentry of his time, was an ab-
sentee landlord, content to leave the running of
his estate to a manager who did not hesitate to
employ his authority to dismiss a man on the
slightest pretext as a weapon of persecution.'

Her proud head drooped, shamed by the sort
of indictment which twenty years previously must
have cost Colt Kielder's father his job. She had
no recollection of her mother, who had died with-

out making any impression upon her infant mind, and only fleeting memories of the father who, after the death of his wife, had seemed to consider his children a burden to be shifted on to any available shoulders—governesses, schoolteachers, servants—while he took up permanent residence in London and salved his no doubt uneasy conscience by paying short annual visits to the family home. His eventual death had left her less moved than the passing of an ancient gander that had been her constant companion all during childhood . . .

'As a boy,' Colt Kielder seemed to achieve insight into her thoughts, 'I could never decide whether you and your brother—the Earl of Falstone—were more deserving of envy or pity.'

The bracketing of the word pity with the proud Falstone name inspired sufficient anger to tilt her chin.

'You've gained the reputation of being an astute businessman, Mr Kielder, a brilliant engineer who formed a small company and then set out to woo lucrative contracts from Middle Eastern oil sheiks, earning a name for ruthless efficiency and at the same time amassing a considerable fortune. Nevertheless, the fact that you're now head of a large international construction company has not earned you the right to patronise your . . . your . . .'

'Betters . . .?' he suggested mildly when she hesitated, seeking a diplomatic alternative.

'If you insist,' she flashed, employing hauteur to conceal a twinge of shame. 'Though you may have gained materially, you seem in the process

to have forfeited all sense of decency, to have cut
the ties of loyalty that have bound you since birth
to this region and to people who were once foolish
enough to regard you as one of themselves.'

When he stepped back a pace she congratulated
herself upon having probed a sensitive nerve, until
a glance over his impassive features quickly dispelled this notion.

'Believe it or not,' he drawled laconically, 'the
welfare of the inhabitants of this area was one of
the motives that influenced my decision to tender
for the contract to build the dam. No one knows
better than I the frustration men feel when they're
tied to jobs they dislike or to employers with
whom they're incompatible, simply because
there's no alternative source of employment in the
area. Also, no other contractor would have felt
the same determination as myself to ensure that
the countryside is restored as far as possible to its
original state once the dam has been completed.
All decisions appertaining to the location of the
dam were taken by area authorities who are
immune to outside influences, but often instructions that have to be implemented by contractors
are open to interpretation, consequently, I
deliberately tendered low, hoping to manoeuvre
myself into a position where I could make sure
that the least possible upset is caused while work
is in progress; see to it that every complaint
receives a fair hearing, and to do everything in
my power to ensure that householders whose
homes are to be flooded receive adequate com-
pensation.'

'How very altruistic!' Rowan flared, her normally gentle nature inflamed by the hypocrisy of the man she felt certain was enjoying the anger he had caused to a member of a family whose position of privilege he had always resented. 'Would you mind telling me how you intend to compensate the otter for being deprived of his holt, or the badger of his sett? Why don't you be honest and admit that you would never have returned to your old home, would have turned your back forever on a region whose best known landmark bears your name, if there had been nothing personal to be gained?'

She felt sickened and unaccountably disappointed by his narrow-eyed start of surprise, by the quirk of annoyance fleeting across a stern mouth that seemed to indicate a stabbing conscience.

'I'm right, aren't I . . .?' she accused, wide-eyed and motionless as the doe whose head had just appeared peeping through trunks of fir trees fringing the forest road.

He hesitated, then squared his shoulders, standing tall and implacable as the Kielder Stone.

'Yes, I did have a personal reason for returning home,' he frowned, 'but it's no secret—indeed, I've imagined that by this time it would have become common knowledge. My advice to you, Lady Rowan,' he continued with a look of pity that caused her a stirring of panic, 'is to seek an immediate showdown with your brother; it appears to me that he's kept his own counsel long enough.'

Kept his own counsel! Persistent as Cello's hooves, the warning drummed into her mind as she sped homeward, leaving Colt Kielder without so much as a cursory goodbye in her anxiety to confront her brother, to wheedle out of him what she suspected might be the latest of a long line of indiscretions. Her frown deepened when Cello veered to canter up the stable drive reaching to the rear of Falstone Castle as she was struck more forcibly than usual by signs of dilapidation and neglect. Massive iron gates inscribed with the motto: *Nil Conscire Sibe*—Having No Remorse— leant drunkenly against crumbling stone pillars; the roof of a once imposing lodge had tiles askew, allowing access to inquisitive pigeons; a shrubbery resembling an unpruned jungle of suckers, dead branches and fallen leaves. Making a mental resolution to begin attacking the flourishing clumps of weeds as soon as possible, she slung the saddle from Cello's back, gave her a good rub down, then saw her comfortably stabled before entering the rear of the castle by way of a huge, old-fashioned kitchen.

At the sound of footsteps upon the stone-flagged floor an elderly woman wearing an ancient ankle-length dress beneath a spotlessly white apron turned round to greet her.

'My, but you're looking bonny today, bairn!' Sharp eyes set black as currants into a face wrinkled as a walnut, glistened with pride as they roved Rowan's flushed cheeks and wild-blue eyes. 'I knew the ride would do you good,' she turned to resume her task of kneading a pile of dough, 'there's nothing helps a body's looks more than fresh air and exercise.'

'Nanny,' Rowan blurted, ignoring the maxim she had heard repeated regularly and monotonously over the years by the old servant who had exerted the only stable influence she had ever known, 'do you know the whereabouts of my brother? I'm anxious to have a word with him.'

'Then you'd better keep your wits about you,' Nanny sniffed. 'He's out at the moment, went roaring down the drive in that nasty red sports car of his about half an hour ago, but he'll be back shortly—he's ordered an early lunch before setting off for London.'

'What, *again*? But he's only just returned!'

'It puzzles me why he doesn't stay there permanently,' Nanny retorted with the assurance of an old retainer, 'because whenever he does come home he mooches around the house with a face as long as a fiddle, hankering after bright lights and entertainment, just as your father did.'

'I hope you don't encourage this extravagance, Nanny,' Rowan chewed her lip. 'Father could afford to live in London, but I'm certain Nigel can't, because it's as much as I can do to persuade him to pay the household bills.'

'What a comedown!' Mournfully, Nanny shook her head. 'To think that not so many years ago there were twenty household servants in this castle, not to mention gardeners, grooms and stable boys—and everyone kept to his proper place. Not like nowadays,' she pummelled aggravated fists into the lump of dough, 'when the son of a Scot—a farm labourer who worked on this very estate—is allowed leave to pretend that Jack's as good as his master!'

Rowan did not pretend to misunderstand. 'Social barriers disappeared many years ago, Nanny,' she reproved gently, 'equal opportunities have put a good education within reach of all. I can find nothing likeable about Colt Kielder as a person, but one has to acknowledge that the man, as well as being clever, is a determined hard-headed business tycoon. And while we're on the subject,' she ventured timidly, knowing the old woman's depth of partisanship for her race, 'don't you think it's rather silly of you to continue adding fuel to feuds that have roots buried hundreds of years in the past? We're living in the twentieth century, for decades English and Scottish Borderers have lived peaceably side by side, so well integrated—even marriage—that it would be difficult to find one family of either nationality who could boast a completely pure strain.'

'*Integrated!*' Nanny swung round to scoff. 'As Colt Kielder's father was integrated! He was a proud man who, every time he lifted his eyes towards the Kielder Stone, was reminded that once his clan had been the most powerful and respected of all the Scottish Border clans, a man who found it difficult to bend his knee, one whose bitterness at having been reduced to accepting a job as a servant on the estate of an English earl was well known to his wife and no doubt to his son. I'm aware that mixed marriages that once were forbidden by law are accepted today as normal, nevertheless, old rancours still linger, under a thin skimming of unity the cracks are still there. Why else,' she challenged fiercely, 'do you suppose that within one Border village two separate accents can still be heard; why does even the smallest community support both an English church and a Scottish chapel, and why do half the regulars of local pubs leave the celebrating of Christmas to the English and save all their energies for Hogmanay? Mark my words well, bairn,' Nanny fixed her with the glittering stare of the fanatic, 'that man has returned to these parts determined to revenge his father's humiliation and to restore the status of a family whose sons are reputed to be gifted with a giant's strength and magic armour! Take care that you're not deceived, by Colt Kielder, whose ancestors' boast is recorded in border ballads:

In my plume is set the holly green
And the leaves of the rowan tree

In spite of the derisory grimace she had directed towards Nanny before leaving her to her own devices, Rowan felt a shiver chasing down her spine as she stepped out of the kitchen regions into a flagged hall with a staircase of stone and arrow-slit windows through which sunrays were slanting upon woven wallhangings depicting tableaux in which English lances lined the Border, provoking Scots to come over to engage in one of the violent skirmishes for which the reivers had been famous; and creeping, shadowy figures—

identifiable as Scots by their cocky bonnets—
making their stealthy way along night-darkened
fells in the direction of cattle herded into pens at
the back of a farmhouse where an unsuspecting
family slept.

Tattered battle standards and family portraits
lined the rest of the walls of a castle built solid as
a fortress, able to withstand the ravages caused by
blazing arrows, so that during the three occasions
when the interior had been gutted by fire the
blackened shell had remained intact and had
immediately been refurbished by the reigning
earl. But now, centuries after the last battle cry
had been heard, time and the elements were
managing to achieve what the reivers had failed
to do—eroding stonework that crumbled at a
touch; obliterating portraits with layers of grime;
rotting oak panelling to the texture of sponge;
reducing once magnificent hangings to shreds—
tattered as Falstone pride.

As Nanny had refused help to prepare the lunch
and housework held little appeal, Rowan made her
way to a shed housing an assortment of gardening
tools, deciding that expending her energy upon
the weed-choked shrubbery might help to take her
mind off Colt Kielder's worrying warning.
Although his remark had been obliquely phrased
its meaning had been clear. Nigel was keeping her
in the dark about something—but what? All sorts
of possibilities presented themselves as she
trundled a wheelbarrow down the drive, but one
by one she discounted them as being too com-
monplace to be kept secret. If ever Nigel had

gambling debts and money was tight the household bills were the first to suffer; if he had at last
found someone among his crowd of girl-friends
whom he wished to marry—fear clawed her throat
as she wondered how she could cope if any new
mistress of Falstone should turn out to be unfriendly—she would have known intuitively, because her brother was always full of high spirits
whenever he fell in love. Lately he had been
moody and irascible. She sighed, then turned her
attention upon waist-high weeds, determined to
clear her mind of useless conjecture.

By the time Nigel's car turned into the driveway
the shrubbery was looking almost respectable, but
her face was streaked from contact with dusty
leaves, and her hair dishevelled, stuck with pieces
of broken twig. Brakes squealed a protest when
he caught sight of her, his fastidious nose turning
up in disgust when he stepped out of the car to
question disdainfully:

'What are you up to, for heaven's sake? Must
you embarrass me by taking over the gardener's
duties?'

'We have no gardener,' she reminded him
gently. 'You said we could no longer afford to
employ him, remember?'

He looked momentarily abashed but quickly
recovered his composure. 'So I did,' he agreed
airily. 'Nevertheless, there's still no need for you
to get into such a disgusting mess. Pretty soon——'
With a sharp snap of teeth he broke off and
swiftly changed the subject. 'Get into the car and
I'll run you up to the house. I must hurry, I have

an appointment in London this evening.'

Once again Rowan felt a fluttering of fear, a premonition that something unpleasant was hovering in the background. Her brother had always been able to dominate her, to quell with a look, but this time she meant to have her say.

'There's something I must discuss with you before you leave.'

Warily, he eyed her stubborn bottom lip, the glint of determination in usually serene eyes. 'I suppose you've heard rumours?' Awkwardly, he shifted his feet and dropped his eyes, reminding her of the schoolboy who had never voluntarily owned up to any misdeed.

'Rumours about what?' she queried stonily. 'Are you suggesting that there's some important family matter about which outsiders are better informed than I am?'

'I don't intend to stand about any longer than I need in this damned chilly air. Get inside the car.' When he swung away in a temper, unable to meet her eyes, Rowan's heart seemed to freeze, rendering mind and senses numb while she was driven up to the house and then ushered inside the hall with the terse instruction, 'Have a quick wash and brush-up, in five minutes I'll join you for lunch.'

Mechanically she went up to her room, grateful that shock had lent her an outward appearance of calm and rendered her unable to think, for she knew that if she did she would begin to cry. She had no illusions about her brother who, over the years, had proved himself to be weak, vain, and outrageously selfish. Yet at times he could be affectionate and kind. Certainly, he had never gone deliberately out of his way to hurt her.

Cushioned by this thought, she made her way down to the dining-room and was even able to muster a smile when Nigel turned from the window at the sound of her approach.

'Shall we eat first and talk later?'

Numbly, she nodded, knowing that food would choke her, yet, in the manner of one who appreciates that a state of limbo has to be endured before the pleasures of heaven or the agonies of hell, she toyed her way through broth, lamb cutlets, and one of Nanny's unnameable puddings. By the time the table had been cleared she felt the peak of her endurance had been reached.

'Coffee . . .?' With a shaking hand she lifted the coffee pot in response to Nigel's nod, then remained poised, frozen with shock, when he blurted:

'I've sold Falstone Castle—I *had* to,' he appealed desperately, 'there was simply no other way I could clear my debts!'

Rowan stared, transfixed with horror, at the thin, aristocratic features of the man who had inherited an ancient title, a descendant of men who had not hesitated to spill their blood in defence of their land, who had fought to the death to protect their home and to retain their children's rightful inheritance.

'You've done *what* . . .?' Her horrified whisper seemed to bounce from the walls of the silent room, even the expressions on family portraits looked shocked, painted eyes fixed upon the shamefaced custodian of their ancient title.

'For heaven's sake, Rowan, there's no need to look like that, it's not exactly the end of the world!' Blustering with temper, he rose to his feet and shoved aside his chair. 'It'll do you good to get away from this Godforsaken place—you've never left it, not even for a day. Personally, I shall feel eternally grateful to Father for insisting upon my being educated at boarding school and for following that up with a two-year commission in his old regiment, because it was during such times that I discovered a world of laughter and enjoyment, a world in which people live, not merely exist!' Suddenly he changed tack and opted for a more coaxing attitude in an attempt to disperse her uncanny stillness, the deathly pallor of a profile that seemed etched from marble.

'You'll enjoy London, Rowan. I'll sell my flat, then once we've found a house in a decent neighbourhood we'll join the jet set for a year-long holiday—sunbathing in Barbados; skiing in St Moritz; shopping in Paris. We'll take in the Cannes Film Festival, then after Wimbledon we'll make for Monte Carlo where with a bit of luck we could be invited to join a yacht for a cruise of the Greek Islands. I promise you, Rowan,' he waxed enthusiastic, 'that in a year from now you won't care a damn about Colt Kielder lording it over Falstone Castle!'

'Colt Kielder . . .!' She dropped into a chair as her knees buckled under her. 'Are you telling me that you've actually sold our home to that . . . that *Scot*?'

'Oh, spare me the histrionics!' Conscience, guilt, or perhaps a mixture of both ignited his explosive temper. '*Yes*, I've sold out to Colt Kielder, I don't give a damn about his nationality, all I care about is the fact that as a multimillionaire he can afford to meet my price.'

He started towards her, alarmed by her look of pain, and stared down at the face of a stranger, a pinched, stricken profile with a fixed look bearing none of the fond tolerance he was used to receiving from his gentle, unworldly young sister.

'*Traitor . . .!*' Her sibilant condemnation startled him rigid and for the first time the enormity of what he had done seemed to impinge upon his conscience. 'For weeks you must have plotted behind my back, sharing meals, sharing the same roof, yet giving not the least hint of your intention. I'll never forgive you this betrayal, Nigel!' she choked on a rush of tears. 'Even Scottish reivers, barbarians though they were, earned themselves the reputation of being honourable enough—whenever they were forced to break bread with their enemies—to place a black boar's head upon the table as a warning that treachery was imminent!'

CHAPTER TWO

CELLO seemed attuned to Rowan's mood as dolefully the mare picked her way towards the valley. Tenant farmers had to be told of the estate's change of ownership; retired servants who had spent a lifetime in the service of the Earls of Falstone had to be informed as tactfully as possible that permanent security of tenure could no longer be guaranteed to the occupants of grace and favour cottages. For days Rowan had baulked at the task ahead, then had been shamed by the realisation that she was falling prey to the same cowardly impulse as her brother, who had dodged unpleasantness until the last possible moment, thereby leaving her vulnerable to the hints of a hateful usurper.

She could have opted for the easy way out, could have faded into the background and allowed Nigel to carry out his intention of sending each of his tenants stiff, formal letters containing the bare outlines of their changed circumstances, but to Rowan most of them were not merely tenants but friends, and friendship imposed upon her a duty to ensure that the news was broken as gently as possible.

Sadly she made her way towards Beck Farm, the home of Tom and Beth Graham and their pretty teenaged daughter Dale, cringing from the thought of taking worry and unhappiness into a household whose welcome was always warm. A strange new sound disturbed the countryside as she headed Cello away from their usual route which was no longer safe for horses and riders. Day by day the main road through the forest— narrow, winding, with deep ditches running either side, fashioned in the days when a pony and trap was the ideal way to enjoy an exceptionally lovely drive with glimpses of a stream tumbling down the fellside and erupting into a thousand tiny cascades as it was confronted by huge stones and boulders stuck fast in the river bed—was becoming choked and churned up by a heavy volume of traffic, huge-wheeled monsters glaring bright yellow against a backdrop of sober forest green; a trailing convoy of earth-diggers; concrete mixers; tunnelling machines; lorries laden with mile upon mile of steel pipe, tools and an unending variety of equipment; caravans intent upon swelling the temporary town that had already grown larger than the village, and private cars packed with tough-looking, horn-tooting men whose enthusiastic race to join in the rape of the valley had been curbed to an irritating crawl.

Mercifully, however, as she rode deep into the forest to make her daily check upon its inhabitants, everything appeared to be as normal—wild goats and deer placidly grazing; red squirrels scurrying about their business; blue and brown hares patently disinterested; red grouse, duck, ravens, woodpeckers, goldcrests, kestrels, skylarks, whinchats, nightjars, dippers, wagtails, snipe and even a rarely-sighted heron all seemed complacently unaware of the atmosphere of destruction threatening their surroundings.

Immediately Cello's hooves began clattering over the cobbled yard, Beth Graham erupted from the farmhouse beaming a smile of welcome.

'The tea's brewed, Lady Rowan. A feeling in my bones told me that you'd be visiting us today.'

'Then I haven't chosen an inconvenient time?' Rowan slid from the saddle and looped Cello's bridle over a convenient post.

'Bless you, no!' assured the motherly woman, who ought to have been favoured with a large brood of children to spoil instead of just one solitary chick and every lonely youngster she could scoop within her orbit. 'As I was saying to Tom only last evening, the mere sight of you brings me comfort, a reminder that if ever we're in trouble you'll always be at hand to sort it out. We're simple folk, as you well know—good farmers,' she claimed without false modesty, 'but babes in the wood when it comes to dealing with people of high authority. Remember how we fretted ourselves silly for weeks, wondering if our farm was to be among those to be submerged by dam water,' she chuckled, ushering Rowan into a spotlessly clean kitchen, 'and how you were able, in a matter of hours, to set our minds at rest?'

'That was more good luck than good management,' Rowan confessed, sinking down into a chair and watching appreciatively while Beth poured steaming amber liquid into her cup. 'On my way home that day I just happened to bump into Colt Kielder, and when I mentioned your worry he promptly supplied the good news that your fears were unfounded.'

'But only at your request,' Beth defended stoutly. 'It appears to me that men involved in affairs of business become so absorbed in the mechanics of their project, especially one as big as the dam, that they're apt to overlook the fears—real or imaginary—of insignificant people such as Tom and myself who suddenly find themselves slap in the middle of the path of progress. I don't know what would happen to us if we didn't have you to rely on!'

Suddenly, the freshly-baked scones and creamy, home-churned butter lost all their appeal. Rowan pushed aside her plate, knowing she could not emulate Nigel's ability to eat, apparently unconcerned, while debating how best to confess to an act of treachery.

Seemingly oblivious to her distress, Beth prattled happily on, turning a knife in Rowan's wound. 'Tom and I have come to the conclusion that the building of the dam might not be such a bad thing after all. You remember my mentioning that our Dale has been pestering us since she left school to be allowed to stay with my sister in Newcastle while she looks for a typing job?'

Mechanically, Rowan nodded.

'Well, that problem has now been solved,' Beth glowed triumphantly. 'Mr Kielder is in need of a junior in his site office and he's very kindly offered Dale the job.'

The mere mention of Colt Kielder's name inflicted intolerable pain; the gratitude Beth was displaying struck Rowan as the ultimate in disloyalty. She jumped to her feet to exclaim in a voice as grating as the sound made by the legs of her chair as they scraped across the sandstone floor:

'Then it's just as well that you approve of Colt Kielder, because shortly he's to become your landlord—the new owner of Falstone Castle and its estate!'

'But, Lady Rowan . . .!' she heard Beth gasp as she ran towards the door, 'does that mean that *you* are thinking of leaving us? *No*, you can't be,' she wailed, 'we need you here!'

By the time she had reached Black Dyke Rowan had had time to reflect and to feel ashamed of her unreasonable attitude. Resolving to apologise to Beth as soon as possible, she tethered Cello to a gatepost and went in search of Tom Graham, determined that this time she would keep her emotions under control, would not allow the mention of Colt Kielder's name to upset the dignity that was expected of a Falstone.

She found him in a barn and was not in the least surprised when, after she had greeted him by name, he merely grunted acknowledgement of her presence and continued forking bales of hay. He was yet another of the Border Scots whose forebears had somehow managed to stray across the Border, settling down and working among English neighbours without ever becoming part of the community.

She began without preamble, expecting no sign of regret at the news of the imminent departure of the Falstones, yet unprepared for the uncharacteristic expression of pleasure that transformed his features.

'I've come to tell you that you're soon to have a change of landlord, Tom. Falstone Castle and the estate have been sold to Colt Kielder.'

Cold eyes flickered with a spiteful gleam. 'My, but that's good news!'

She flinched from the deliberate snub and in spite of her vow to remain calm an indignant rejoinder spilled past her lips.

'It puzzles me why any Scot should choose to live on the English side of the Border!'

'Me, too,' he glared, setting his shoulders in the stance of an adversary.

'Then why . . .?' she faltered, nonplussed.

'When my family settled here this land belonged to Scotland,' he glared fiercely, 'and in spite of what's written in the Statute Book in my eyes it will always remain so. For centuries ownership was disputed between England and Scotland, so much so that it earned the title of the Debateable Land, and since neither side would admit to responsibility for clashes between English and Scots settlers it came to be regarded as outlaw country, a place where the rich and powerful came to grab as much land as they could.'

'Are you implying that my family——' Rowan began angrily.

'I'm implying nothing,' he interrupted with a

scowl. 'The truth of what I've said is recorded in our family Bible, together with the threat that a curse will fall upon any member of a Scottish family who gives ground to the thieving English! For years I've been greatly angered at having been forced to pay rent to a foreign landlord,' he hissed, eyeing her with a gleam of fanaticism, 'but thank God the tide has turned once more in favour of Scotland and once again a Kielder is to be king— and every reigning monarch has need of a castle!'

More shaken than she had ever felt in her life before, Rowan backed out of his presence, appalled by an antagonism that she had never dreamt existed, by the realisation that beneath a thin veneer of civilisation lay the old resentments, rancour and bitterness that had existed between ancient Border clans.

Exhausted as if she had done battle, she heaved her slight, quivering frame into the saddle, tempted to set Cello on a course for home. But the impulse was checked as subconsciously she drew upon the courage and determination inherited from ancestors whose strength had made them great, whose motto *Having No Remorse* had been made applicable not only to their enemies but also to themselves.

Dusk was falling by the time she had finished her round of scattered cottages and trotted into the stable yard at the rear of the castle. She slid from the saddle, physically exhausted by miles of riding, emotionally drained by hours of wheedling, reassuring, and cajoling, by the woeful, watering eyes of pensioners who had served her family well and who now looked to her for guidance. As mechanically she attended to Cello's comfort, their many bewildered questions echoed in her ears.

'If you leave, who will look in on us when we're taken badly?'

'Who'll write my letters to my grandson in Canada?'

'Who will we get to fill in forms and collect our pensions?'

'How will we contact the doctor . . . the chiropodist . . .'

Hating Colt Kielder, placing the entire blame for their distress upon his self-assertive shoulders, she left Cello quietly munching oats and, dispirited to the verge of tears, she slipped into the castle through the rear entrance. As she passed the kitchen she noted with relief that it was empty—Nanny's chatter would have been more than she could have borne at that stage—so she hurried towards the solitude of the library, intent upon curling up to brood inside one of the capacious, shabby armchairs.

The doorbell pealed when she was halfway across the hall. Impulsively she quickened her steps, hoping to gain the sanctuary of the library without being noticed, and had almost achieved her aim when she was shamed by Nanny's spear of acid humour.

'As you're obviously in an unsociable mood, shall I get rid of the caller, whoever he might be?'

'Yes, please, Nanny,' she blushed, defensive as

a reprimanded child. 'I've heard enough of people's troubles for one day. Unless,' she added the afterthought, 'our visitor brings news of importance—I'll leave you to make your own judgment.'

The wide curved back of an armchair seemed to open arms wide to receive her when she slumped into its embrace and leant her head against a wing of padded leather. She closed her eyes, revelling in an atmosphere of deep repose, until her peace was invaded by the sound of squeaking hinges when Nanny thrust open the door to announce dourly:

'The Cowt insists upon seeing you!'

Rowan shot upright, appalled by the ungracious introduction and by Nanny's ability to register dislike by making the pronouncement of a name sound offensive. Blessing the foresight that had led her to keep the old servant in ignorance of their changed circumstances, she jumped to her feet, prepared to apologise for Nanny's disgraceful show of truculence.

But Colt Kielder looked quite unabashed as he sauntered in Nanny's wake, one corner of his mouth curled upwards as if tugged by a ghost of amusement. 'I'm sorry, Mr Kielder,' she began stiffly, 'Nanny finds it difficult to pronounce some words properly, I'm afraid.'

Her breath caught as if severed, when unexpectedly he smiled. 'Please don't apologise for reviving pleasant memories of the past, Lady Rowan. My mother used often to call me Cowt, which is the traditional Scottish pronunciation of our family name.'

'I'm well aware of that fact!' Nanny bridled. 'Cowt means "strong"—it's no coincidence that the largest and most outstanding boulder in the district has been endowed with the name given to every firstborn Kielder male.'

When she flounced out of the room, Rowan shrugged, then turned her attention to her visitor, only to be further annoyed by his cool, disparaging appraisal of his surroundings.

Every reigning monarch has need of a castle! The reminder of Tom Graham's words prompted a spurt of uncharacteristic sarcasm.

'Well, Mr Kielder, I need hardly ask the reason behind your visit. You seem impatient to begin a survey of your new domain.'

She regretted the statement the moment it was voiced—regretted the return of flinty hardness to clear grey eyes; the stiffening of facial muscles; the arrogant tilt of a head capped with hair as darkly-sheened as his mood, as fiery as hidden temper. As she could not afford to offend the man from whom she wished to beg a favour, she strove to rectify her mistake by making an immediate apology.

'Please excuse my lack of manners, Mr Kielder. I've no doubt that you called in the hope of speaking to my brother, who unfortunately has not yet returned from London. However, now that you are here, there's a personal matter I'd like to discuss with you. Won't you please take a seat?' She fluttered nervous hands in the direction of a chair. 'May I offer you tea . . . or a drink, perhaps?'

'Neither, thank you, Lady Rowan.' When he sat down the massive armchair seemed to assume Lilliputian proportions. 'As a matter of fact, I came specifically to see you.'

'To see me?' She looked blank. 'But why . . .?'

'I'll explain later, once we've disposed of your problem. Fire away . . .!'

A blush rose to her cheeks. Made timid by a brusqueness that shredded the already tattered Falstone pride, she sank back into her chair and with lashes lowered, fingers twisting nervously in her lap, confessed in a whisper:

'I hate the idea of living in London. I want to stay here to look after Nanny—I'm all the family she has. Unfortunately,' she husked, then swallowed hard to clear her throat, 'finding suitable accommodation is proving very difficult. People whose homes are due to be flooded are leaving the district because there are no houses available, so I was wondering whether in the circumstances . . .' she hesitated, lashes quivering madly as the wings of an agitated moth, '. . . you would consider allowing us to occupy the Lodge—for a suitable rent, of course?'

Bravely she lifted her head to stare wide-eyed with panic when for a cruel length of time he silently deliberated, his grey-eyed glance cooling the heat in her cheeks, his lack of response dampening her hopes and setting the final seal upon her humiliation.

Mortified, she withstood his scrutiny, a helpless butterfly impaled by the critical eye of a collector, then drooped with despair when instead of relieving her misery he mused obliquely:

'Destiny must be on my side. Wasn't it Shakespeare who wrote: "There's a divinity that shapes our ends, Rough-hew them how we will?"' When her only response was mute bewilderment, he enlightened her, 'I sought this meeting in order to put to you a proposition which I suspect might supply the solution to your problems as well as my own. Interior decorating is hardly my strong point, and when I move in here,' his glance slewed around the room, 'I shall need the help of someone possessing discrimination and impeccable taste in order to ensure that any curtains, carpets, or furniture beyond repair are replaced by items perfectly attuned to their surroundings. Also, as I intend to do a certain amount of entertaining I shall need a hostess as well as a secretary to cope with any problems arising from the estate and its many elderly tenants. In short, Lady Rowan, I'd like the castle to be run as smoothly and efficiently as I run my business, a place that I can come home to and relax without having to face any extra burden of responsibility.'

Rowan felt a stirring of hope—was he about to offer her employment?

In spite of her desire to have the situation clarified, curiosity prompted her to pry:

'What attracted you to Falstone Castle in the first place—surely a smaller establishment would have been more convenient for a man in your position?'

Dusk was crowding the ancient room, filling it with shadows that veiled his eyes and set his profile into a mould that appeared dark and brooding.

'It may surprise you to learn that for me this place is full of reminders of my childhood,' he astonished her by saying, 'of days when my mother who was employed as a sewing maid used to smuggle me up the back stairs so that she could keep an eye on me while she darned and patched the household linen, sewed buttons on shirts, and carried out invisible repairs on your own childish frills and flounces.'

As if the memory had touched a painful nerve, he rose to his feet and began prowling around the room. When he hesitated in front of the window Rowan saw a muscle twitching in his cheek as he fingered heavy velvet curtains that had hidden in their folds repairs that had been skilfully executed many years previously.

'One of the greatest ironies of life must be the way monuments are erected to fools while others less famous but of greater worth are denied even a modest inscription on a tombstone.'

'Your mother is dead?' she ventured timidly, sensing a turmoil of regret behind an expressionless exterior.

'Both my parents lost their lives in a flood that sent houses bobbing like matchboxes upon a swollen river.' His cool, matter-of-fact tone took her completely by surprise. 'It happened two years after our arrival in America. I was staying with a school friend at the time, and returned the following day to discover that I had no home, no parents, not even the slightest possession to remember them by.'

He must have recognised pity in her choked gasp, a small cry of distress for a young boy left stranded in a country full of alien faces, left to forage for himself in early adolescence, a time when the help and encouragement of loving parents is imperative. Suddenly his tough insensitivity seemed understandable—even forgivable—in a boy who had suddenly had to become a man when a man was needed.

'Don't overburden your tender heart on my account, Lady Rowan.' To her chagrin he sounded lightly amused. 'The grounding I received as a boy living in temporary accommodation sited wherever dams, factories or power stations happened to be being built later proved invaluable. Having personal knowledge of the art of survival when constructing concrete jungles has helped me to understand the stresses that occur when men are herded together, living in primitive conditions, has enabled me to appreciate their points of view whenever work has been disrupted by conflict between workers and management. It has also taught me that in order to earn a man's respect a boss has to be capable of carrying out any task he expects his workers to do, to be able to roll up his sleeves and pitch in whenever an extra pair of hands would come in useful. The Earls of Falstone would have done well to have learnt a similar lesson,' he mocked. 'It might have enabled them to hang on to their inheritance.'

Rowan stiffened, resentful of this mild criticism of her family, yet too honest to deny the truth of his words. 'Both my father's and brother's management of the estate may be open to criticism,' she admitted coldly, 'but there is a lesson you could learn from them, for it appears to me that in your fight to achieve riches you've overlooked the importance of knowing how to relax. But perhaps you haven't yet achieved your ultimate aim, Mr Kielder,' she lifted her head to direct a faintly contemptuous stare. 'Money may have bought you a castle, but you're probably in the process of discovering that money can't buy prestige or love.'

She trembled into silence, wondering if she had gone too far, comparing the uncanny stillness pervading the atmosphere with the sudden cessation of birdsong in the forest, the freezing of all animal movement that always preceded the boom of an explosion in the valley below.

His voice was controlled, yet her sensitive nerves warned of danger, the sort of eruption that can be expected when volcanic lava is rumbling beneath a cap of ice. 'I find relaxation boring, I'd far rather be outside mixing in from the touchlines, in the areas that interest me. Neither prestige nor love is included in my catalogue of interests.'

'And yet you're not an aimless person, Mr Kielder,' she tilted bravely. 'Like every other ambitious man you must have some goal. To what do you attribute the drive mechanism behind your dramatic rise to power?'

'To revenge, I suppose,' he admitted with a trace of transatlantic drawl. 'Specifically, revenge upon the English Establishment, a bunch of toffee-nosed snobs, bastions of the so-called upper class, who attempt to perpetuate the belief that they are a separate entity by spelling their names differently and by pronouncing their vowels in a way that suggests they're attempting to speak with a mouthful of plums!'

Her sensitive nature recoiled from a look of disparagement that seemed to indicate that he considered her a fully paid up member of this exclusive club.

'Then presumably,' she croaked, 'as you appear to have lumped all members of the nobility into one despised race, the guests you plan to entertain will be mainly business men?'

'Then you presume wrongly,' he contradicted smoothly. 'With the help of your brother, whose co-operation with my plan was one of the conditions imposed when I agreed to relieve him of his debts, I intend to become accepted by the establishment, to gain entry into their tight circle of snobbery, thereby exorcising an inherited resentment of flaunted superiority by proving that English imperiousness is mere propaganda put about to disguise the real truth, which is that an Englishman's loyalty and allegiance can be bought—quite cheaply.'

Rowan sat rigid in her chair, feeling seared by a whiff of white-hot heat, sensing the presence of a furnace of resentment stoked up behind a cast iron door of indifference.

'Well, Lady Rowan,' his impatient voice jerked her out of her trance, 'what do you say, are you prepared to co-operate?'

Indignation drove her to her feet, gave her the courage to confront him face to face when she flared:

'Prepared to conform to your outrageous theory, don't you mean? No, Mr Kielder, whatever my brother may have led you to believe, I, at least, am not for sale, so you can peddle your offer of employment elsewhere!'

'Employment . . .?' Both his tone and expression registered utter astonishment. 'Whenever I need workers I contact an employment agency. You've obviously misunderstood me, Lady Rowan. What I'm asking you to do is marry me.'

CHAPTER THREE

FOR the better part of two days Rowan had ridden Cello along forest trails, wrestling with emotions that were a tangle of anger, indignation, astonishment, and an overriding sense of worry about Nanny's future. To leave her alone without so much as a roof over her head was unthinkable, yet it was a foregone conclusion that the old lady would refuse to leave the area in which she had been born and where in a quiet churchyard moss-covered headstones tilted by subsidence, their inscriptions almost obliterated by the elements and the passage of time, recorded the last resting places of relatives who had defended the frontier against marauding Scots, members of a family of whom it had been said they '*Would rather lose their lives and livings than break the code of the Border by going back on their word*'. But in spite of a reluctance to upset Nanny's familiar world, the time had eventually arrived when Rowan had decided that she could not dodge the unpleasant task a moment longer.

When informed of the sale of the castle Nanny had taken the news as Rowan had expected she would, first of all biting deeply into a quivering bottom lip, then immediately assuming the mien of a tough Borderer used to weathering a lifetime of calamities. However, her reaction to the news

41

that she had turned down Colt Kielder's impudent proposal of marriage had struck Rowan as shocking and totally unpredictable.

'Silly child!' she had snapped fiercely. 'How could you be foolish enough to let slip an ideal chance to gain revenge, to make the arrogant Scot pay dearly for trying to emulate his betters!'

Rowan tried to blank from her mind the incredible conversation that had followed, but as Cello picked her way along a bridle path Nanny's words seemed sighed upon the breeze, whispered insidiously through the branches of rustling pines. For the umpteenth time she recalled her own highly indignant response.

'Are you actually suggesting that I ought to have *accepted* the man's outrageous proposal?'

And Nanny's uncompromisingly swift affirmative. 'Certainly I am! Not for the first time, it's fallen to one of the female line to uphold Falstone pride, to fight to retain possession of family property. There are more ways than one of skinning a rabbit!' she had hissed the blunt Border maxim. 'Some battles are fought with dirk and sword, others with cunning and guile. You owe a duty to old and needy tenants as well as to ancestors who sacrificed everything, even their lives, to ensure that the Falstones retained their rightful heritage.'

'But the castle has already been sold, Nanny!' Rowan had protested. 'Legal formalities have already been completed, so there's no way that I can cancel out the harm my brother has done.'

She had been alarmed by the wicked, almost

witchlike look that had distorted Nanny's face at the mention of Nigel's betrayal.

'Every generation spawns a weakling,' she had muttered. 'Whenever the runt of a litter is the firstborn, the strength of the remainder must compensate for his weakness. Your brother was no match for the Cowt—the Strong Man—but by marrying Kielder you can ensure that Falstones are never ousted, that the line continued to flourish in the family home!'

Wearied by the argument that had raged unceasingly over the past two days, Rowan dismounted to allow Cello a peaceful graze while she sat on the bank of a stream and unwrapped the sandwiches she had packed in a cowardly effort to avoid being served lunch by Nanny whose continuous pressure was becoming unbearable.

But churning emotions had dispelled her appetite and after forcing down a couple of mouthfuls she broke up the remainder of the sandwiches and cast them into the stream before stretching out on the grass. With her hands clasped beneath her head she gazed blankly at a patch of blue sky just visible above the crowns of forest giants, striving to subdue quivering nerves, attempting to discover a route towards sanity that would bypass the path of duty that Nanny had insisted must be trod.

'Other Falstone women married for money whenever family fortunes were low ... The motto: "Having No Remorse" is not merely a pretty inscription, but a vow that commits every Falstone to weathering the pain caused by guilt or bitter repent-

*ance, to overcoming their reluctance to commit a
wrong or to act cruelly whenever conscience conflicts
with family interests . . .'*

Persistent as water pounding against stone,
Nanny's edicts drummed through Rowan's mind.
Even when heavy eyelids drooped, weighted with
weariness, she was haunted by dreams of a church
filled with wedding guests divided into hostile
camps by a narrow strip of aisle; of a bridegroom
whose head was supporting a copper-red crown;
of a bride slowly approaching an altar wearing a
shimmering dress which, immediately her bridegroom took her hand, became transformed into a
suit of glittering armour!

Lashes flew up over wide-awake eyes when she
became conscious of a piercing whistle close by.
Instinctively she froze, recognising the call of an
otter making contact with its mate. Then the
sound of splashing drew her attention towards the
stream and she was treated to the rare sight of a
chocolate-coloured male otter with small, bright
eyes set into a flattened head sporting prominent
whiskers, propelling himself underwater, employing his long, thick, tapering tail as a rudder.

'Don't move!' a voice urged softly in her ear.
'If we're very lucky his wife might decide to join
him—perhaps even their young.'

It required tremendous effort of will to obey
Colt Kielder's command. Not even the novelty of
watching a rare sighting of the usually nocturnal
animal that shunned people and ventured out of
his riverside holt in daytime only when he thought
himself unobserved could temper the shock of his

presence, or the embarrassing realisation that he must have stolen up stealthily from behind and remained watching over her while she slept.

As she obeyed, stiff with resentment, a female otter appeared out of nowhere and slid down the river bank to begin a teasing flirtation with her mate in the water. Gradually, imperceptibly, Rowan's tension gave way to delight as for several enchanting minutes she watched a ballet of grace and strength as the otters postured, preened, bent, stretched, reared, dived, darted and glided, obviously revelling in the freedom of movement obtained from water, their natural element.

When, after a final dive, the pair disappeared beneath the surface, she expelled a long-held sigh of contentment—a contentment that was suddenly dispersed by a mocking reminder of Colt Kielder's presence.

'Every courtship should be as carefree and lighthearted. They've probably now departed to the privacy of their holt to mate or merely to cuddle close together and enjoy tender, affectionate exchanges.'

Swiftly Rowan scrambled to her feet, unnerved by an ambience of intimacy that was intensified by his lazy, narrow-eyed appraisal of her scarlet cheeks and wide blue eyes reflecting awkward shyness.

'I wonder if there are any cubs?' She rushed into speech, conscious that strange, intense undercurrents were causing her to babble wildly. 'Because cubs are born blind they're restricted to the holt for the first ten weeks of their lives and

they call out for their mother in a very loud penetrating squeak if they think she's been absent too
long. They swim instinctively, of course, but
mother has to duck their fat furry bodies under
water to encourage them to dive.'

'Are you really unaware, Lady Rowan, or have
you merely forgotten,' he rocked on his heels,
looking amused, 'that a great deal of the first
twelve years of my life was spent in this forest
studying wildlife, first in the company of my
father who taught me all he knew, then later alone,
foraging, tracking and keeping watch.'

'Also laying traps and snares, I've no doubt!'

For the life of her she could not resist the impulse to snap, feeling as sensitive to the menace
of his towering frame as a chicken to a marauding
fox.

She stared defiantly at the man whose tall,
rangy frame clad in denim trousers and checked
shirt seemed to epitomise power, whose grey eyes,
when they were not guarded, could take on the
hardness of bedrock, the flint-sharp core of earth
left exposed on the floor of the valley where his
monstrous yellow earth-gobblers had gorged
layers of grass and rich topsoil. She blanched
beneath the weight of a look that threatened to
crush her disdain as boulders hacked from the
quarry were crushed into gravel, then felt even
more intimidated when he smiled, a smile that
recalled out of the deep recesses of her mind a
lesson learned in the schoolroom: '*Some maintain
that smiling has its origin in facial gestures adopted
by our primitive ancestors to prove that their teeth*

were at rest and not tensed for an attack upon an enemy's throat!'

'You resent like hell my presence here, don't you, Lady Rowan?' he tilted gently. 'What a pity your attitude is being copied by the rest of the locals who've been conditioned over the centuries to following where Falstones lead.'

'Did you expect us to welcome your intrusion into our peaceful lives?' she flashed, her knees buckling with fright. 'Can you give me one good reason why we shouldn't resent the noise caused by your armoured divisions making an assault upon our land; why we should enjoy being turned out of our homes, having our roads choked with traffic, our villages stormed every Saturday night by troupes of hooligans in search of diversion? You will never be accepted here!' Bravely, she jutted her chin. 'Though our land has been invaded, we're determined never to fraternise.'

'In other words you're set upon making life as difficult as possible for all of us.' Impatience lent to his words an extra sardonic steel. 'As usual, what has been deemed best by the Falstones has had to be accepted as being best for everyone. You wish to remain an elitist minority, wrapped within a cocoon of selfishness and solitude that renders you immune to the pressures and needs of society. You sneer at my men, implying that they're an army of renegades bent upon rape and pillage, whereas in actual fact they're a bunch of tough guys, dedicated to their work, who accept the need to live in primitive conditions and in return expect others to tolerate their need to relax and enjoy themselves for just one night out of seven.

'I could give you many reasons why the building of the dam is essential,' he growled, 'the main
one being a vital shortage of water in a country
whose population keeps growing. The quantities
of water used by industry are so huge as to be
almost incomprehensible. The bed you sleep in,
every item on your table and in your household,
needed water somewhere in the course of its pro-
duction. Water is needed for drinking, for growing food, for washing ourselves and our belong-
ings—we simply couldn't live without it—yet,
obviously, if the Falstones had their way, house-
wives would once again be reduced to the back-
breaking task of collecting water from rivers and
wells in buckets. You, and others who think like
you, seem quite prepared to ignore the hardships
imposed by lack of water, the increasing instance
of disease, providing your outlandish, mummified
existence is preserved!'

'Mummified . . .!' she croaked, outraged, feeling battered by his hail of scorn. 'We do have
access to television, radio, and newspapers, Mr
Kielder!' Her attempt to sound withering was
foiled by her wobbling tone. 'The fact that we're
kept so well informed about the happenings in
the outside world has made us all the more determined to opt out of it!'

'But at what cost?' he drawled, switching
suddenly from antagonism to gentle mockery as
his amused eyes slid over slim thighs encased in
ancient riding breeches and the swell of cur-
vaceous breasts obscured by a shapeless sweater.

'How long is it since you wore a skirt, Lady Rowan? If I might hazard a guess, I'd say it was the day you abandoned gymslips.'

She could have fought argument with argument, fire with fire, scorn with scorn, but the softly jeering question left her gasping, pride decimated.

'It must be true what they say about women dressing solely to please men,' he continued, cocking a derisory eyebrow. 'Perhaps now that there's a surplus of eligible males in the area my men will have less reason to complain about the dowdy lack of appeal in the female population. As most local girls will follow wherever you lead,' he maintained with a deceptive idleness that blunted the impact of his words, 'it will fall to me, as your fiancé, to claim the privilege of supplying you with a decent wardrobe.'

His cool assumption that she was prepared to accept his proposal had the effect of a douche of cold water upon her fiery cheeks, draining her of colour until her face looked pinched, her wide blue eyes appalled. Confident that it was ridiculous to feel so panic-stricken, assuring herself inwardly that no man could be as all-powerful, as all-conquering as he appeared, Rowan tightened her grip upon flustered nerves and attempted to spell out clearly and coldly:

'I wouldn't marry you if you were the proverbial last man in the world! While the dam is still under construction, I know I shall find it difficult to avoid your company, but believe me, Mr

Kielder, I shall try exceedingly hard to ensure that I see as little of you as possible for the remainder of the time you're here!'

A spark flickered in the depths of grey eyes, then was just as suddenly extinguished. 'Falstone Castle was purchased as a permanent home, not just as a temporary retreat,' he reminded her almost kindly. 'There'll be plenty of work for me to do here, long after the dam has been completed. As a matter of fact, its completion will mark the beginning of a scheme I have in mind to renew life and bring prosperity to the area.'

'What sort of scheme . . .?' Surprise tilted her head erect, as if alerted by a battle cry warning of the approach of thieving Scottish reivers.

'I visualise a vast recreational area.' Her heart plummeted to the soles of her small boots. 'A place where facilities will be provided for sailing, water-skiing, rowing and angling, with a modern clubhouse where the hundreds who I'm certain will flock to the area each weekend can have their hunger and thirst assuaged. Bird hides will be situated in appropriate spots for any whose hobby is birdwatching, and nature reserves and wildlife sanctuaries will be created for those who enjoy less energetic pursuits. Picnic areas will be needed to cater for the needs of families with young children; nature trails to attract school parties, and later on,' he paused, seemingly immune to the look of horror on his listener's face, 'all cottages remaining above water level will be modernised and rented out to holidaymakers during the summer season.'

'You don't mean it!' she croaked through a dry throat. 'You surely don't intend to deprive our oldest tenants of their homes—some of them are in their eighties, they would be heartbroken if ever they were forced to move!'

His callous shrug struck her as appalling. 'One mustn't allow sentiment to interfere with one's judgment, especially when one is planning a commercial venture as huge as the one I've just outlined,' he told her in a tone totally devoid of compassion. 'The welfare of family retainers must remain the responsibility of your brother and yourself—it's most certainly not mine. Once the Falstones move out of the Castle, so far as I'm concerned their commitments leave with them. As I've already pointed out, I have no intention of shouldering further responsibilities. In any case,' he consoled her as a seeming afterthought, 'once your tenants have been served notice to quit, the local council will feel bound to offer them alternative accommodation.'

'Miles away,' Rowan accused fiercely, 'in a place full of strangers, out of sight and sound of everything and everybody they know and love!'

Once again, his smile brought a reminder of unpleasantness long past, of days when his outlaw ancestors had added the word 'blackmail' to the English language.

'The remedy lies in your own hands, Lady Rowan,' he confirmed that her thoughts had done him no injustice. 'Any marriage between a Falstone and a Kielder is bound to unite families who have kept feuds simmering for centuries, must help to wipe out the vendettas and petty jealousies that are rife in the area because of traditional Anglo-Scottish antipathy.'

Rowan wanted to flee, but her feet felt pinned to the ground; yearned to reward his cold-blooded attempt to blackmail with some vicious act of retribution. The ancient curse of the reivers was already forming on her lips—*May your soul go straight to the fire of hell!*—when a chill encompassed her body, suspending all speech, thought and action.

A ghostly whisper from the past seemed to fill her ears; *'Desire for revenge spans even eternity! At times the act can be accomplished with the satisfaction and speed of a swordthrust through the heart of an enemy, but at other times it must be a subtle, ingenious, meticulously-planned, carefully-executed art!'*

When she addressed Colt Kielder her voice sounded strangely disembodied—as if some cold unemotional being had sublimated her will and was forcing an incredible promise through her stiff lips.

'On your own head be it, Mr Kielder! A man who lacks honour holds a distinct advantage at the bargaining table, and so, although you're an unscrupulous rogue whom I dislike intensely, it appears that I've been left no choice but to gamble on the chance that marriage to you may turn out to be fractionally less distasteful than a lifetime spent with a tormented conscience.'

CHAPTER FOUR

Had she really promised to marry Colt Kielder?

As Nanny helped her to search through cedar-wood chests packed with curtains, tablecloths, bedlinen and many ornate satin, taffeta, silk, cotton and lace dresses lovingly packed and preserved by Falstone wives during previous decades, Rowan was frantically asking herself if she had suffered a brainstorm, if she could perhaps extricate herself from an intolerable situation by pleading that she must have fallen victim to some kind of mental aberration and should therefore not be held responsible for her impulsive acceptance of his proposal.

'Ah, here it is!' With a groan, Nanny emerged triumphant from the depths of a chest and straightened her aching back to display a shroud of white muslin draped over one arm. 'If you'll pass me the scissors I'll snip the stitches from the bottom of this bag,' she prompted. 'We'll soon find out if your grandmother's wedding dress is still wearable.'

Without the slightest quickening of interest, she did as Nanny asked, then turned to stroll across to the dusty attic window. It was February, the month of spring flowers in some parts, but high up on the fells snowflakes were being tossed in a wind that was wailing and sighing around the ancient castle walls—like a mournful ballad, Rowan thought, gazing sightlessly over the fells and forest, streams and farmland the Falstones no longer owned—a sad dirge bemoaning a battle lost, the demise of a proud, once influential family.

'It's yellowed a bit with age.' Rowan half turned when Nanny stepped towards her. 'But the material seems sound enough and the embroidery is still perfect.'

When she held out the dress for inspection a breath caught in Rowan's throat as she eyed a shimmering fall of satin, aged to the deep creamy shade of buttermilk, its high rounded collar and swirling hem encrusted with tiny seed pearls formed into garlands of exquisitely pale English roses. The bodice, tightly pintucked, arrowed down towards a waistband that looked too incredibly narrow to accommodate any healthy human form, and long tight sleeves that fell into points below the wristbands seemed to call out for hands so small, white and slender that instinctively she clenched her weather-tanned fists and thrust them behind her back.

'Will it fit, do you suppose, Nanny?' She pursed doubtful lips. 'Grandmother Falstone appears to have been more wraith than human.'

'A wraith that produced six healthy sons, went horseriding every spare hour avail˄ble, entertained frequently, and ensured that the household was run like clockwork,' Nanny chuckled grimly.

'And was she happy?' Rowan pondered wistfully. 'Were she and Grandfather very much in love?'

'Love!' Nanny snorted with derision, displaying a hard intolerance of sentiment that was typical of her Border breed. 'In those days love was considered to be the least important ingredient of a suitable marriage, the most vital qualities a man looked for in a wife were a healthy body capable of bearing sons and a hefty dowry to help maintain them.'

'And what about women?' Rowan challenged with interest. 'What did they most hope to find in a husband?'

'Kindness, I dare say . . .' Nanny hesitated as if surprised by the notion that women should be considered entitled to an opinion, 'and of course a title was a must so far as the gentry were concerned. But otherwise,' she shrugged, 'a woman could count herself fortunate if she found herself wed to a man capable of restraining his temper and exercising discretion in his infidelities.'

'Big deal!' Rowan scoffed. 'You make even Colt Kielder sound a good catch.'

'Compared with some of the previous Earls of Falstone, I dare say he might be,' Nanny snapped, squaring her shoulders to ease the stiffness of rheumy bones. 'In spite of their renowned strength, Kielder men have never been known to beat their wives, so be grateful for small mercies, my girl; at least when you marry him you'll have the satisfaction of knowing you've done all in your power to right your brother's wrong. It was your bounden duty to ensure the well-being of your tenants—surely their happiness is reward enough without hankering after love as well!'

Rowan was still biting her lip with vexation when she strode towards the stables, trying to feel grateful for the fact that as Colt Kielder's wife she was unlikely to be beaten! She would not have felt so angry, so impotent in her arguments, had she not known that Nanny's outmoded, servile attitude towards marriage was upheld to a greater or lesser extent by most of the women in their community.

Their outlandish, mummified community!

Unwilling to admit that there might be even a grain of truth in Colt Kielder's sarcastic remark, she concentrated her mind upon the task of saddling up Cello before mounting swiftly and urging the mare to gallop off as if all the furies of hell were snapping at her heels.

Prompted by habit, she made her way towards the Kielder Stone, the high vantage point that supplied a view of silent, majestic forest, gently sloping fells and sparkling crystal water that could always be relied upon to act as a panacea for jangled nerves. She had reached to within a couple of yards of the boulder before spotting the figure of a man standing so motionless he seemed to have merged into the stone. Immediately she recognised Colt Kielder she jerked upon the reins, intending to veer Cello in the opposite direction, but recognition was mutual, and when he addressed her she felt she had no option but to pull Cello to a standstill.

'I know this stone is purported to possess magical properties so far as my family is concerned,' he gave it an affectionate pat, 'but I was not prepared to be pleasantly rewarded quite so quickly.'

'Would you be prepared to test the legend's grimmer side, by riding widdershins three times around the stone?' she challenged coldly.

'And risk becoming the target of some unmentionable evil? No, thank you,' he grinned, 'I don't believe in tempting providence. Besides which, the sun is in the wrong position to allow me to ride widdershins—by which I presume you mean against the sun?'

When he held out a hand to help her from the saddle she looked the other way, pretending not to have noticed.

'You claim to be in sympathy with the modern world,' she charged, 'yet you appear wary of challenging the truth of the legend.'

'Are you daring me to?' The amused question aroused her curiosity.

Swiftly she turned her head towards him so that blue eyes collided with determined grey. 'No, you mustn't! The plea escaped her lips without conscious volition, betraying a superstitious dread of retribution that caused his darkly burnished head to toss with astonishment.

'So you really do believe that harm would befall me were I to ignore the legend of the Kielder Stone?' For once he seemed too preoccupied to jeer.

'I . . . I don't know . . . I'm not certain,' Rowan stammered, a blush of embarrassment running wild in her cheeks, 'but I think you would be foolish to deliberately challenge fate.'

With a speed that left her gasping he plucked her from the saddle and set her gently on the ground in front of him. With his strong grip burning into her waist, holding her steady, and his head lowering fiery as a torch towards her troubled face, he jested softly:

'Kielder men were said to wear plumes of rowan leaves in their helmets because they believed that by doing so they gained immunity to evil. With you as my talisman, Lady Rowan, I dare anything . . .!'

Every bone in her body seemed to melt when his bright reiver's head drew closer. Slowly, positively, he slid his hands around her waist and drew her forward until she was pinned against his powerfully pounding chest. Her young, untried lips began to tremble, anticipating the assault of a hard mouth that looked determined to the point of cruelty, then she experienced a gamut of unfamiliar emotions when a tremor weakened his tightly leashed body and she sensed intuitively—as if the message had sped straight from Eve—that his swiftly-indrawn breath, the tight grip of his hands against her waist, spelt danger—that he was tempted to anticipate the pleasures of marriage without the benefit of a clergyman's blessing!

Later, she was often to wonder what the outcome might have been had her bemused eyes not fallen as if in search of guidance upon the mass of heather-crowned sandstone with deep channels stained red—legend swore with the blood of bygone Kielder victims.

Uttering a gasp of self-loathing, she tore out of his embrace, sickened by the realisation that she had almost bent to the will of a member of a clan whose ability to charm was reputed to be as great as its thirst to dominate, a family that had been responsible for introducing into the English language the word 'blackmail'—black rent—the illegal extraction of money from tenants and farmers in exchange for unasked-for and unwanted protection.

'Don't touch me!' she cried out when his hands reached out to reclaim her. '*Thieving, plundering reiver . . .!*'

Immediately he froze, his face expressionless as a mask, a dull tinge of colour rising beneath his tan.

'For heaven's sake, Rowan,' he clamped, 'when will you come to terms with the fact that you're living in the twentieth century? The deeds of the reivers belong in the history books, and that's exactly where they should be allowed to remain.'

'Family characteristics don't change,' she accused, eyes bright with unshed tears. 'How dare you treat me like a camp-follower, one who is prepared to tolerate the crude advances of a rough renegade! Must you class all women alike,' she gritted, 'or are you simply too insensitive to notice that some of us are different?'

Lightning flashed in cloud-grey eyes, the air fairly seemed to crackle around his fiery head as for frightening seconds he fought to harness his temper. Then suddenly tempest gave way to hail, a cold cruel shower that burst over her head, leaving her gasping.

'Yes, Rowan, you're certainly different from the majority of your sex—unique in your timid immaturity! My men have been warned that hunting and even birdwatching have been banned in certain parts of the area that are known habitats of protected species, examples of wildlife so rare they are in danger of becoming extinct. It would now appear—if your reaction to my friendly advance can be taken as a criterion—that a clause must be added to the effect that the female population of this area must also be included in the veto!'

Friendly advance! The searing imprint of his hands upon her body, the weakness of her limbs, the screaming disarray of newly-aroused senses, gave lie to the understatement.

'It's not we who are culturally retarded,' she tilted. 'After decades of fighting off the invasions of unscrupulous rogues, of being forced to take part in bloody and bitter battles in defence of our property, civilisation was welcomed with open arms. Whereas the aims of yourself and your gang of intruders appear to be identical with those of deliberately-destructive, coarse-mannered, pillaging reivers. It's a very long time,' she concluded shakily, 'since families in this area were last called upon to lock up their daughters!'

Colt made no attempt to argue, did not even bother to look her way when she stumbled over to Cello and heaved her shaking limbs into the saddle. She left him standing still and forbidding as the stone that bore his name, gazing north across the Border—glorying, no doubt, she decided bitterly, in the fact that ownership of the land he was surveying could no longer be disputed because once again a Kielder was king!

A noise that intruded as a murmur gradually developed into an ear-splitting roar as she approached the rim of the valley and looked down upon miles of black earth flattened by bulldozers, dozens of yellow monsters belching poisonous smoke from their exhausts as they scoured the earth, scraping closer and closer down to the bedrock into which piles had to be driven before the actual building of the dam could begin. From her vantage point, the men appeared like a nest of yellow-helmeted worker ants, scurrying and burrowing, too intent upon progress to care about the trail of destruction left in their wake.

On impulse, she urged Cello towards a dirt road that led towards a quarry where a collection of huts had been erected. Beth Graham had mentioned that her daughter, Dale, had begun working in one of the collection of huts that had been utilised as a temporary office, and suddenly it seemed imperative that the youngster should be put on her guard, to ensure that her ingenuousness was not exploited by the gang of bare-chested roughnecks who were yelling disrespectful exchanges across the width of the valley in coarse Celtic accents.

When the road petered out she left Cello tethered to a nearby tree and began descending narrow steps hewn out of the face of the plateau in order to gain access to the base of the quarry.

Three mechanical monsters were burrowing into loose rock, gulping stone into huge shovels, then swivelling round to deposit each load into waiting lorries. Clasping her hands to her ears to deaden the noisy din, Rowan gulped in a lungful of air, then held her breath as she ran unnoticed past the scene of activity towards the comparatively clean and quiet spot where the huts had been situated.

When the door of the nearest hut flew open she tried to check her speed, but the impetus of her flight was so swift she stumbled and catapulted forward into the arms of the man who had stepped over the threshold.

'Whoa!' He rocked on his heels at the impact, but quickly recovered and grabbed her arms to steady her. 'I'd heard mention that the folk that live hereabouts are renowned for their wildly passionate natures, still I wasn't prepared for the pleasure of having the prettiest girl around throwing herself straight into my arms.'

'Please forgive me . . .' Stiffly, she stepped out of his clutches, mistrusting the amused, transatlantic drawl that immediately labelled him a Kielder ally. 'I'm looking for Dale Graham,' she frosted. 'Perhaps you can tell me where I might find her?'

Thick eyebrows drew together in a frown—obviously, Colt Kielder's handsome young colleague, dressed immaculately in a pale blue safari suit and fringed buckskin boots, was unused to being given the brush-off by a member of the opposite sex. 'Sure I can—she's inside.' He jerked a nod in the direction of the hut he had just left.

'Let me take you to her.'

'No need, as she's near I'll find her myself. But thank you all the same, Mr . . .?'

'McCabe . . . Abraham McCabe,' he supplied eagerly, 'but please call me Abe.'

'Thank you, *Mr* McCabe,' Rowan stressed pointedly. 'Now if you'll excuse me,' she tried to edge past him into the hut, 'I'd like to speak to Dale, if you don't mind?'

Good humour bounced back into his face like the proverbial rubber ball. 'Of course I don't mind! And to prove that our company's policy of being friendly and co-operative with the natives is no mere boast, I insist upon escorting you to her myself.'

Oblivious to her annoyance, he placed a hand under her elbow and propelled her inside the office. 'Dale, you have a visitor, Miss . . .' he hesitated, then cocked an enquiring eyebrow at the girl whose pale blonde head had lifted from a typewriter when they entered the office.

'Lady Rowan!' she gasped, rising to her feet to greet her with a smile of welcome. 'Mother was fretting only last night about the time that's elapsed since you last visited her.'

'*Lady Rowan* . . .!' Abe broke in thunderstruck. 'Why didn't you say you were Colt's intended? I sure am delighted to meet you, ma'am—we were all convinced that the boss would be content to go on adding numbers to his book until he was ready to draw his pension! Telephone numbers . . . date book,' he enlightened when she looked puzzled. 'We all have one. Travelling guys need to know where they can pick up a chick in a hurry whenever they arrive at their various destinations!'

When a frozen silence fell, a glance at Rowan's patrician profile, stiff with disdain, and Dale's flush of embarrassment made him suddenly aware of his gaffe. 'Heck, I'm sorry if I've spoken out of turn, Lady Rowan,' awkwardly he poked at a crack in the linoleum with the toe of his fashionable cowboy boot, 'I guess I'm just not up to consorting with royalty.'

This elevation of status was too much for Rowan's sense of humour. A dimple sprang to existence at the corner of her mouth as she tried to suppress a smile, and when Abe grinned engagingly she gave up the struggle and dissolved into laughter.

'Merely a member of the lesser nobility, I'm afraid,' she corrected with a gurgle, 'as far removed from royalty as I hope I am from farmyard fowl.'

'You're such a fool, Abe!' Dale's casual admonishment, the fond, almost flirtatious glance she shared with the young American caused Rowan's tone to sound several degrees cooler when she requested:

'If you don't mind, Mr McCabe, I'd like to speak to Dale in private.'

'Surely,' he grinned, 'but only if you'll promise to drop the Mister and call me Abe?'

'Very well, if you must hold me to ransom . . . Abe,' she squashed, reverting to disdain.

Overawed by an air of quiet authority inherited

at birth but seldom exercised, he backed out of the room mumbling some excuse about his presence being required in the quarry. But when they were finally left alone Rowan found it difficult to put into words her concern for Dale's safety.

'Won't you please sit down, Lady Rowan?' Dale sounded defensive, almost as if she had guessed the reason behind her visit and was resentful. Without preamble, Rowan took the plunge.

'I don't think your parents can be aware of the type of personnel employed by the Kielder Company,' she began tentatively. 'As your home is rather isolated, I suppose news of what's happening in the valley has been slow to reach them. I'm certain, however, that once they've been told about the prevailing atmosphere they'll be quick to advise that you look for more suitable employment.'

'The prevailing atmosphere is just great, Lady Rowan.' Dale jumped to her feet, spilling heated words of protest. 'The men working on the dam aren't paragons of virtue by any means, they curse hard, work hard and play even harder, nevertheless their conduct in my presence has been irreproachable—indeed, their attitude is so protective I'm often led to wonder whether they see me as an infant rather than a responsible seventeen-year-old. *They* won't allow me to grow up, but you must, Lady Rowan,' she pleaded, her eyes liquid with the threat of tears. 'I love my work—so much that I can't bear the thought of being forced to leave!'

'But are you sure that it's the work that attracts

you?' Rowan swept a glance over office equipment filmed with dust, spartan furniture, and bare, comfortless walls. 'Mr McCabe's forceful personality could be very appealing to an impressionable young girl,' she suggested pointedly.

'I won't pretend that I don't enjoy his company,' Dale tilted. 'He and his fellow workers have brought new enthusiasm and a capacity for enjoyment that's been sadly lacking in this valley. Not everyone in the area agrees with your views, Lady Rowan,' she dared to challenge. 'My friends all agree that the building of the dam is the best thing that's happened here for decades. People will come to look at the new dam and discover that human beings exist here—that it's not merely a sanctuary for wildlife in danger of extinction!'

Rowan stared, at a loss to understand how she had managed to remain so completely out of touch with the views of a generation only slightly younger than herself. She was just about to probe deeper when Dale, embarrassed by her outburst, rushed towards the door, flinging a nervous apology across her shoulder.

'Please excuse me, I've just remembered a telephone message that ought to have been passed on to Abe.'

'It's time I was leaving, anyway,' Rowan told her hastily, 'I've taken up enough of your time. But I would like to continue our discussion, Dale. Perhaps you could suggest a time and place that would be more convenient?'

'Would you like to be shown around the quarry before you leave, Lady Rowan?' To her annoyance, Abe loomed upon the threshold, his untimely interruption allowing Dale the opportunity she had been seeking to escape. 'Would you mind wearing this?' he extended a yellow protective helmet towards her. 'The boss is very strict about conforming to safety regulations.'

He could have said nothing more calculated to arouse her resentment, to make her determined to gain one victory, however insignificant, over Colt Kielder and his brash young deputy. If she had refused point blank to wear the helmet he could have argued his point, but when she stepped past him, ignoring both the helmet and his request, he looked completely nonplussed.

'What is the purpose of that machine?' Provocatively, she walked across to a machine standing momentarily idle, curious about the working of an attached conveyor belt leading up to the rim of a tower.

'It's a crusher,' he told her, then pleaded desperately, 'Lady Rowan, would you *please* put this helmet on?'

The quarry was wrapped in silence; some of the men were sipping mugs of tea, others were leaning from the windows of their cabs chatting amicably, but the sound of grit crunching beneath the tyres of an approaching car, the squeal of brakes and the slamming of a car door had the effect of galvanising the entire workforce into action. Suddenly the crusher sprang into noisy life and the conveyor belt began moving its load of rock towards the top of the tower where it toppled over and fell with a horrible grinding noise on to huge churning blades. A loud crash sent Rowan spinning round, wide-eyed with fright, to see a heavy steel ball swinging from a chain on the end of a jib smashing large boulders into pieces.

She felt it was entirely appropriate that Colt Kielder should choose that moment to step into her line of vision. He looked coldly furious, in an obviously filthy temper.

'Why isn't Lady Rowan wearing protective headgear?' His yell stabbed through noise being made by a complete orchestra of machinery.

'Er ... she was just about to put it on ... the men have just this minute recommenced working,' Abe stumbled, his young brow creased with anxiety.

'*You're fired!*' Colt Kielder snapped, his expression flinty as the gravel spewing out of the crusher. 'It's your responsibility to ensure that safety regulations are observed—there's no room in this company for any man who's proved himself incapable of carrying out orders.'

'That's most unfair!'

'Gee, Colt, if you'd only give me a chance to explain ...!'

'But, Mr Kielder, it wasn't Abe's fault!'

Simultaneously, Rowan, Abe, and Dale voiced a protest to Colt Kielder's unyielding figure as he stalked back to his Land Rover, then shared appalled glances when without turning his fiery head he disappeared from sight.

'Don't worry, Abe.' Ridden with guilt, Rowan tried desperately to comfort the shocked youth. 'When he hears my explanation he's bound to change his mind.'

'I wouldn't bet on it,' Dale cautioned, bleakly condemning. 'Before coming to work here and seeing for myself how ruthless he can be, I used to scoff at my mother's tale about the traditional rite once said to have been performed at all Kielder christenings. Every male child,' she gulped, wide eyes betraying that she was not as immune as she had professed to Border mythology, 'had his right hand excluded from the ceremony in order to ensure that in time of feud his enemies would be destroyed by the strength of his unblessed hand!'

CHAPTER FIVE

IN spite of Nanny's arguments to the contrary Rowan felt certain, as she stepped over the threshold of the tiny woodland church and began her slow walk up the aisle towards her waiting bridegroom, that no other Falstone bride, however threatened, could have entered into marriage with the same amount of dread and resentment in her heart.

The scene was like an extension to her dream: oak pews crammed to capacity with two warring factions—puzzled locals who had looked upon her as the champion of their cause and who were now feeling that she had let them down, and a deputation of off-duty workers from the enemy camp looking uncomfortably spruce and out of place, as they returned stares of defiance across the narrow dividing aisle.

As she approached the altar steps on her brother's arm a weak ray of sunshine began moving across a stained glass window donated by some previous Falstone earl and played upon her bridegroom's head so that his burnished hair took on the appearance of a fiery crown. Then as she stood quaking by his side, waiting for the ceremony to begin, it began progressing steadily across the inscribed glass, picking out each jewel-bright word so that they felt seared upon her forehead: *Having No Remorse!*

She had remorse in plenty—remorse at having been forced to strangle her pride and go in search of the autocratic company boss to explain the circumstances that had let to Abe's dismissal and to beg him to rescind his decision.

For the first time in their acquaintance his look had been cold and distant when, after following his tracks around the perimeter of the dam, she had finally spotted the empty Land Rover and saw him a few yards distant conversing with one of the site foremen. She had dismounted and stood nervously fondling Cello's muzzle, waiting to be noticed, and had quaked in her shoes, nervous as a delinquent employee expecting a rocket from her boss, when finally he had strode towards her.

She had sensed past aggravations seething beneath a surface of politeness when he had enquired. 'Do you wish to speak to me?'

'Yes, please, if it's convenient,' she had gulped.

Mortified, she had watched him flick back his cuff to study his watch before conceding: 'I have ten minutes to spare, if that length of time will suffice?' In response to her nod, he had then suggested, 'Let's walk into the forest where the noise of machinery is not quite so persistent.'

After ascending a slope topped by a belt of forest green they had plunged into a depth of silence, an interior reminiscent of the peace of a centuries-old cathedral, a place whose shell had withstood the desecration of many battles, the ravages of change, while miraculously retaining its core of

serenity. A resinous incense had risen from the
carpet of pine needles crushed beneath their feet
while they had walked without speaking until a
felled tree trunk had seemed to indicate an ideal
spot to rest. Rowan had sat down, expecting Colt
to join her, but instead he had propped one foot
on the tree trunk while, using his knee as an arm-
rest, he had stood lowering.

'I want to speak to you about Abe,' she had
begun nervously.

'In which case, you can save your breath,' he
had cut in sharply. 'I never go back on a decision.'

'Not even when you discover that the decision
is an unjust one,' she had burst out furiously, 'that
you've totally misread the circumstances leading
up to it? Abe tried desperately hard to persuade
me to wear a helmet, but for reasons of my own I
chose to ignore his request. No doubt, in his position, you would have resorted to force, but fortunately for me your deputy is not yet fully
indoctrinated with Kielder ruthlessness. The
blame is entirely mine—if your ego demands some
show of retribution for disregarding orders, then
I'm the one who should be punished.'

'You would enjoy that, wouldn't you, Rowan?'
he had leant to jeer, 'would welcome having a little
extra weight added to your self-imposed burden
of martyrdom—an attitude you carry like a banner
of protest against intrusion into your solitude.
Believe me, you're not alone in enjoying the
pleasure of a peaceful read, of a calm, reflective
interval spent pondering upon nothing in par-

ticular, of a quiet ride around the countryside. But solitude should be a chosen, short-lived contrast to being surrounded by convivial company, not a retreat from the world, the sort of retirement you embrace like a nun. Everyone needs a partner in life to argue and row with, to tease and have fun with, to kiss, make up, and make love with. So why fight the inevitable, Rowan, why not try to enjoy my company instead of displaying antagonism on every conceivable occasion—even to the point of rebelling against the minor issue of wearing a protective helmet?'

She had jumped to her feet blazing resentment of his patronage, of the easy, relaxed way he had straightened his tall frame until she had had to tilt her head to glare into his expressionless face.

'You chose your simile well! If I act like a martyr it's because I feel I'm being persecuted for defending my principles. Even birds are free to choose their own mates, yet I'm being forced into marriage with a confirmed bachelor full of lust, a man determined to further his ambitions but who will most likely continue living the life of a debonair tomcat even after he's married. However, your morals—or lack of them—are of no consequence. All I want is your promise that you'll meet two further conditions.'

'Which are . . .?' he had questioned thinly.

'Firstly, that Abe is reinstated,' she had quivered, 'and secondly, if you still insist upon subjecting us both to the indignity of a farcical marriage, that there'll be an absolute minimum of fuss and hypocritical rejoicing attached to the actual ceremony.'

'*Do you, Rowan, take this man to be your lawful wedded husband . . .?*'

The atmosphere inside the church felt as cool as the surrounding walls when she hesitated, forcing herself to remember the well-being of elderly tenants; the future preservation of the countryside she loved; Abe's reinstatement to the job he had lost through no fault of his own, before whispering a shaken: '*I will . . .*'

She suffered the rest of the ceremony in a state of limbo, as detached as a newly-departed spirit hovering above the heads of mourners at her bedside. Even her husband's kiss made little impression upon lips frozen into the semblance of a smile, and it was not until they had left the church and were being driven back to the castle that she was shocked back to reality by Nigel's breezy acceptance of a situation she was finding intolerable.

'I say, what a super car! I'd love a Silver Cloud, but the manager of my garage tells me my name's way down on the waiting list.' He sounded completely devoid of conscience, immune to any feelings of guilt at having shattered the lives of all who depended upon him, then leaving her to pick up the pieces.

'No doubt you'll be returning to London as soon as possible?' In spite of her own silent condemnation, Rowan's hackles rose, recognising thinly-veiled contempt in Colt Kielder's tone when he returned Nigel's friendly overture with a comment that was tantamount to an order.

'Er ... well, I had planned on staying overnight.'

'But wisely changed your mind when you realised that there's really nothing to keep you here,' his new brother-in-law concluded smoothly. Showing characteristic disdain for protocol, he had dismissed the chauffeur and elected to drive the car back to the castle himself, and as Rowan watched his capable hands manipulating the controls she felt dominated, as helpless as any border lass at the mercy of an abducting reiver. 'You'll join us for lunch before you leave,' he negligently commanded Nigel. 'Because Nanny was outraged by our decision to dispense with the customary large wedding reception I'm certain she'll attempt to redress the balance by offering us something rather special.'

'What about the rest of the wedding guests? Won't they be expecting some measure of hospitality?' Nigel sounded shocked.

'Their needs are being catered for at this very moment in the village hall,' Colt told him briefly, 'also a dance has been arranged for later this evening. My wife and I,' he paused as if to savour the words, flicking a glance over Rowan's pale, wan features, 'will join them for the traditional cake-cutting ceremony in order to allay any doubts that we're indifferent to the importance of the occasion. After all,' his tone developed the trace of transatlantic drawl Rowan had learned to interpret as a danger signal, 'in spite of having a few personal differences still to be resolved, for

the sake of good community relations we must try
to live up to the newlyweds' image of passionate
devotion.'

She flinched from an undertone of savagery, yet
managed to find solace in the sight of knuckles
showing white as he gripped the steering wheel—
an indication that her frozen acceptance of the
inevitable was edging his patience near to bedrock, a flaw in his armour that she was quick to
file away in her memory, to be resurrected as a
future weapon of defence.

For some unknown reason Nanny had decided
to serve lunch upon a table set amid the austere
splendour of the baronial hall, a place where stags'
heads leered glassy-eyed from the walls, where
suits of armour with grisly weapons clutched in
mailed fists skulked in shadows being cast by
flames leaping out of the heart of spluttering logs
piled into the centre of a stone fireplace that in
days gone by had housed a spit large enough to
accommodate whole roasted oxen.

With a gesture of distaste that caused her husband to frown, Rowan discarded her flimsy veil
and headdress before slipping into a seat at the
foot of a table set with fine lace place-mats,
highly-polished silver, odd crystal goblets and
remnants of a once-impressive dinner service
gleaned from the depths of dusty cupboards in an
obvious attempt to impress the new owner of
Falstone.

'Hell, Nanny,' Nigel muttered irritably, eyeing
the steaming soup tureen she had placed in the
centre of the table, 'you'll have to offer something

better than broth in exchange for forcing us to suffer the discomfort of gale-force draughts blowing around our ankles!'

'It isn't broth, it's cockie-leekie,' she snapped, 'made with onions and best boiling fowls. And to follow, there's poached salmon with cucumber, then venison cutlets seasoned with herbs, so I'll expect you to clean your plates!'

'All that's required to turn this meal into a real Scottish repast are oatcakes, whisky and the skirl of bagpipes,' Nigel sneered, soured by Nanny's seemingly treacherous shift of allegiance. 'You're acting like a tartan patriot, Nanny, yet I can remember an occasion when I heard you expressing regret that the law forbidding marriage across the line had ever been repealed!'

'True, but times and circumstances change,' she glared. 'I'm older now and too wordly-wise ever to expect law to govern nature. In any case, no true Borderer would ever seek permission to go courting, they've always taken what they wanted and said hang the consequences. Even with their backs to the wall,' her black eyes condemned, spearing his shell of hauteur, 'men of true grit always refused to be routed, wouldn't give one inch of ground, much less a castle, for all the devils in hell!'

Nigel froze her with a look that held none of the tolerance and affection owing to the old woman who had devoted her life to two motherless children, who had not begrudged one minute of the time she had spent nursing them through childhood illnesses, who had sympathised with their woes, consoled them in sorrow, rejoiced in their happiness, the woman whose fanatical devotion to the Falstones and especially to the newest earl made her bitter criticism all the more surprising.

'I think you've said enough, Nanny! Since when have the opinions of servants been either welcomed or tolerated in this household?' Nigel withered caustically.

Her bravado sagged beneath the weight of authority in his tone; her mouth puckered as she tried to still its trembling and a network of lines deepened so that she seemed to age suddenly before Rowan's shocked eyes. She was just about to speak up in her defence when Colt's dangerous drawl forestalled her.

'Since I took over, I expect.' He put Nigel firmly in his place. Then, in case his change of circumstances still had not registered, he spelled out cruelly: 'When you sold your birthright, Falstone, you forfeited all the privileges that went with it. As you appear to be suffering from the delusion that you still wield authority in this household, may I remind you that as from today you are merely a guest here and as such you will be expected to accord to Nanny the respect and deference she has earned by years of devoted service. And now,' he flung down his napkin with a gesture of finality, 'as you have a long journey ahead of you may I suggest you make an early start? Once the renovation of the castle has progressed far enough to allow us to accommodate guests I'll be in touch.'

Rowan's cheeks burned with embarrassment and pity for her brother when awkwardly he took leave of them at the head of the castle steps, his dazed eyes glancing upwards at the crumbling masonry of crenellated walls and twin circular towers, then sliding down to linger upon once-grimacing gargoyles, their expressions now rendered pleasant by erosion, that peered down upon visitors arriving at the front entrance by way of a flight of stone steps hollowed by the footsteps of generations of callers—some friendly, others not—as if conscious for the very first time of the enormity of his loss.

'Goodbye, Rowan.' When he leant to kiss her a suspicion of moisture filming his eyes made her dislike of Colt Kielder soar.

'Goodbye, Nigel dear,' she gulped. Then as she returned his hug she drew him closer to whisper in his ear: 'Don't blame yourself too much—we haven't been completely routed, there's still one Falstone remaining in the castle!'

'Have you forgotten already, or has it not yet registered that you're now a Kielder?' As Nigel's car disappeared down the driveway her keen-eared husband put an arm around her shoulders to lead her back into the hall. When a violent trembling seized her his expression sharpened with concern. 'You're frozen—come closer to the fire.'

Without protest, Rowan allowed him to urge her towards the fire leaping furnace-hot up the stone chimney and stood with her head bent, eyes downcast, while Colt massaged warmth into her frozen limbs, sliding his palms along her back, shoulders and arms until her body began pulsating with thousands of tiny nerves leaping in response to tender, almost seductive strokes.

'You wear purity like a suit of armour, Rowan,' he murmured huskily, devouring her frozen beauty with eyes fired by the lick of reflected flame. 'You were an unbelievably lovely bride. For the rest of my life I shall remember my first sight of you walking towards me down the aisle, your slender body trembling beneath a sheath of satin, pale as your small solemn face, with vivid blue eyes and a mouth glowing ripe and moist as rowan berries behind a veil of early morning mist. Even now, as I feel you quivering beneath my hands and see your very kissable mouth mere inches away, I'm finding it hard to believe that at last I possess the rare and distant being that has haunted my memory since childhood.'

Deliberately, inexorably, his arms tightened to draw her stiff, shocked figure into a close embrace. 'Once,' he husked, feathering a kiss across her brow, 'you challenged me to be honest and admit that I would not have returned to my birthplace had there been nothing personal to be gained.' He hesitated, his eyes fastened hungrily upon soft lips quivering around a gasp of surprise, before astounding her further. 'I decided then that it was too soon to admit that *you* were my motive, that the thought of returning home, in a position to claim Lady Rowan Falstone as a bride, was the goal that forced me to grit my teeth and persevere whenever the going got tough, that made all the sweat, toil, agony and despair of the intervening years worthwhile!'

Grey eyes blazed with a sudden leap of flame seconds before his mouth plunged upon hers, drinking deeper and deeper, as a wanderer lost in the desert would gorge upon the sweet, cool waters of an oasis that for once had not turned out to be a mirage.

Numbed by the shock of his brutal confession, confused by the pressure of steely limbs thrusting hard and unyielding as a blade against her satin-sheathed body, Rowan was swiftly overwhelmed, defeated by a maelstrom of emotion that forced an agonised gasp of protest past her lips—but leaping, treacherous response from her captive body.

Swords, lances and leering stags, tattered pennants, muskets and shields kaleidoscoped above her head when she was lifted into his arms and carried in triumph up the wide stone staircase and along a gallery leading to a passageway lined with many closed doors. He lifted his mouth from hers just long enough to urge:

'Tell me, which is our room?'

The request acted as a lifeline to sanity which she seized in trembling hands.

'Put me down, please, Colt.'

The calmness of her tone, the ease with which she had spoken his name, lulled him into a mood of complacency. Gently he lowered her to her feet and stood smiling, waiting for her directions. Panic was the ally that helped to co-ordinate shaking limbs into a movement so swift he was caught completely off guard when she slipped inside her bedroom, slammed shut the door, then turned the key in the lock with a loud, decisive click.

'*Rowan!*' She backed away in fear from the thud of fists upon the heavy door and from the anger evident even through a barrier of solid oak. 'Don't be foolish—you can't run away for ever from the responsibilities of marriage!'

'A marriage of convenience,' she called back in a terrified treble, '*my* convenience, not yours! You resorted to blackmail and extortion as a means of getting a wife, you *bought* me, just as you bought my home, but believe me, Colt Kielder, a castle and a wife *in name only* were the only Falstone possessions up for sale!'

CHAPTER SIX

'WILFUL child!' Nanny snapped. 'You ought to know better than to pit your wits against the Cowt of Kielder, the last remaining member of a family whose pride in its ability to overcome opposition is legendary.'

'I have pride, too!' Rowan turned upon the old woman whose persistent show of allegiance towards the enemy seemed little short of treachery. 'Too much pride to even contemplate sharing a room, much less a bed, with a man who's made no secret of the fact that he married me simply to prove to himself that he's capable of attaining what appears to be unattainable.'

'As you married *him* in order to retrieve what appeared to be irretrievable!' Nanny countered triumphantly, 'so my advice to you both would be to call an armistice and settle down to making the best of a bad job. You're not the first Falstone bride to have married without love, but you appear determined to be the first to renege upon the solemn vows to love, honour and obey! Colt Kielder isn't likely to allow his line to die out, he's bound to want an heir, therefore I can see nothing but trouble ahead if you persist in refusing to move into the bridal suite, the rooms which for centuries have been reserved for the exclusive use of the master and mistress of Falstone.'

Tense as a bowstring, Rowan stared out of the window, turning a defensive back against Nanny's condemning eyes while nervously she licked her tongue around suddenly dry lips, trying to weather the impact of words that had forced her to realise how incredibly naïve she had been. It had simply never occurred to her that Colt Kielder would expect more than a matrimonial façade, a wife that could be displayed like a pennant to prove his power over the superior Falstones—but Nanny's confident statement, together with his surprising assault a couple of hours ago, had lent her a glimpse into a future that promised to be far more distasteful than she could possibly have imagined. To be legally bound was bad enough, but to be physically bound, to become just another scalp added to the collection he had strung around his belt, was too humiliating to be borne.

She swung on her heel, startling Nanny with a firm, decisive order. 'Put those clothes back into the wardrobe—all except the brown dress, I'll wear that this evening.'

Nanny was so shocked she almost dropped the pile of clothes she was waiting to transfer into the main suite of rooms situated at the head of the passageway.

'What . . . that old thing!' Her scandalised eyes probed through Rowan's modest collection of garments in search of the offending article. 'But you haven't worn that dress for years—you even admitted that buying it was a mistake, that the colour doesn't suit you!'

'Exactly,' Rowan nodded agreement. 'As my

husband seems convinced that women dress solely to please men, I intend to prove him wrong.'

'He won't be pleased,' Nanny warned sharply.

'I'm sure he won't,' Rowan smiled, bolstered by the memory of a ghostly whisper from the past instructing her upon the subtle, ingenious, meticulously-planned, carefully-executed art of extracting revenge. 'King Kielder wants a wife who'll add a pearl of respectability to his stolen crown—unfortunately for him, he's about to discover that the jewel he bought is faceted with thorns!'

Trying to appear unmoved by Nanny's disapproving looks and muttered forebodings, she began preparing herself for the ordeal of facing critical tenants and bold-eyed workers in the company of her new husband. With the deliberate aim of subduing her natural beauty, she skewered wings of raven-black hair into a tightly constricting bun, then puffed a cloud of face powder over dark eyebrows and lashes so that, when the surplus had been brushed away, delicately arched wings and sooty rims were rendered inconspicuous. Leaving her bloodless lips untouched, she slipped into the drably-coloured dress with a hem that because of its immediate loss of favour had been left too long, then, suppressing a squirm of vanity, she laced on a pair of sturdy brogues that added clumsy weight to small feet and detracted from the shapeliness of slender, finely boned ankles.

Nanny's aghast look supplied sufficient proof that her efforts had been rewarded with success.

'Lord save us! You look pale as a ghost,' she

gasped, 'a frumpish ghost that no man in his right mind would take to his bed! You're a wicked, conniving creature,' she accused, but with a glint of admiration and a quirk of amusement softening the stern set of her mouth. 'If the Cowt should decide this evening that his bride deserved a thrashing then I for one will bury my head beneath the bedclothes and leave you to reap your just deserts!'

'Now you're being foolish!' Rowan scolded, feeling her heart lurch. 'I married an ambitious schemer, a ruthless, blackmailing rogue, but not, I think, a sadistic barbarian.'

Yet in spite of her brave assertion her heart was beating a tattoo of trepidation as she descended the stairs and felt the unnerving stillness of the shadow-filled hall—its gloom relieved only by one malevolent red eye of slowly dying embers—rising up to meet her. Her attention was caught by a moving patch of shadow that slowly materialised into the tall figure of a man who could have stepped from a previous century—a man wearing kilt and plaid with a weft and sett so distinctive that the tartan immediately stamped him an inhabitant of the Borders. His swordbelt and sporran, his bonnet, hose, brogues, brooches and buckles were of a quality expected of a clan chief, one of the born leaders of men whose skills were tested against the best among the sporting, hunting, and fishing members of his clan, who was expertly trained in the use of weapons, and whose word was paramount, his honour jealously guarded.

'How good of you to finally put in an appearance!'

She was startled by the discovery that the words were not mouthed by some phantom spirit but had been gritted from the lips of her impatient bridegroom, and had to struggle to associate pride of birth and loyalty to heritage with the man who, in spite of his history, seemed best suited to his image of abrasive, hardheaded business man.

'You startled me!' she choked. 'For a second I thought . . .'

'. . . That you were seeing a ghost from ages past?' he countered grimly. 'This outfit belonged to my father, and to his father before him; I was asked to wear it tonight as a special favour to an old and faithful friend of my family. At first I wanted to refuse, but upon reflection I decided that it would do no harm to demonstrate to Falstone followers that the clan system is still surviving strong and healthy in the Borders, and will continue to supply proof of the adage: *What is in the blood must come out!*'

His dominance was frightening, yet somehow Rowan managed to tilt scornfully: 'Such sentiments sound hypocritical coming from the lips of a man who professes to despise inherited positions of privilege and authority.'

'No clansman bends under the yoke of serfdom,' he countered with a scorn that was damning. 'In place of the feudal system favoured by the English, we Scots share a warm kinship and are honoured by the knowledge that every man is considered to be as good as his chief in battle and in peace.'

Feeling suddenly chilled, Rowan stepped nearer to the fire and stretched her hands towards the glowing embers. When his breath hissed against her ear she drew back her head and saw grey eyes flashing with ferocity as he studied her appearance. Silently he began a thorough examination that scoured her cheeks red and seared a trail of contempt down to the soles of her shuffling feet.

'So . . .!' he deduced, displaying an insight into her thoughts that ripped her naked of assurance, 'you've decided to turn our marriage into a battleground, with your husband as the enemy! So be it, sweet foe,' he conceded almost kindly, 'but I give you fair warning—you're in danger of handing to your enemy the means for your own destruction!' He waited for some response, but when none was forthcoming he snapped a command that jerked her shoulders erect. 'Return to your room and put on your wedding dress—our guests will be expecting to see a radiant bride and, whether by the use of force or persuasion, I intend to ensure that they're not disappointed.'

She found it a galling experience, having to react to his note of authority, having to take orders when she was used only to giving them, but the slight stress he had placed when referring to her bedroom had indicated that he was teetering on the edge of a further skirmish for which she felt ill prepared. So, acting upon the principle that discretion is the better part of valour, she backed out of his menacing presence and fled to her room to carry out his order.

The festivities were in full swing when they entered the village hall, its interior made almost unrecognisable by masses of out-of-season flowers which, together with a buffet table running the full length of one wall, piled high with a delectable assortment of food ranging from small dishes of potted shrimps covered in butter and spiced with mace, huge fresh, pink-fleshed salmon, herrings pickled in vinegar, cold roast turkeys and chickens, sirloins of beef, pork with crackling, boiled legs of lamb and rounds of haggis, to fruit cake and pastries, shortbread, oatcakes and a varied selection of cheeses, must have cost someone a small fortune.

The floor in the centre of the room held a crush of dancers who were evidently finding the toe-tapping music of pipes and drums, clarsach, accordion and fiddle irresistible, and watchers crowding around the dance floor were adding a happy babble of sound that was a mixture of many different accents: softly-lilting Gaelic; the harder Lowland tones, rich in feeling, strong in character; and the louder, heartier voices alien to the area coming from tough, weather-hardened men, spruced up for the occasion in checked shirts and denims, who formed Colt Kielder's army of invaders.

The sight of these men pushing and elbowing their way through the crowd in search of partners, arrogantly filching the youngest, best-looking and most impressionable girls from under the noses of less belligerent locals, aroused Rowan's simmering resentment to boiling point.

'You promised a minimum of fuss!' she flared at her unrepentant husband. 'I was expecting to make a short appearance at a quiet social gathering, not this . . . this . . .'

'My men are citizens of the world,' he reminded her, showing not the slightest trace of compunction. 'In America, for instance, a gathering of this size would be classed as a modest little shindig. In any case,' her nerves reacted with a leap to the return of his lazy drawl, 'from where I'm standing your friends appear to be making the most of an opportunity to let their hair down. Why don't you follow their example, Rowan?' His hands clamped upon her waist, delaying their entrance by pulling her back inside the small, dark no-man's-land that separated the front entrance from the main body of the hall. 'If there's any truth in the saying that matrimony ought to begin with a little aversion, then we should be set on course for a highly successful marriage,' he muttered roughly, the closeness of his lips taking her breath away, 'but for the next couple of hours let's try to sink our differences. Though friendship may still be a little out of our reach, we can at least pretend a state of armed neutrality!'

As his words registered, appealing to both heart and reason, tension left her and she settled suddenly still within the circle of his arms. With the sound of merriment in their ears and a host of friends waiting to greet them, his request for a truce seemed far from unreasonable. He gave her time to ponder, content to watch conflicting expressions of doubt and decision chasing across her sweetly-solemn face. Within their oasis of solitude the sound of silence seemed gradually to smother all other intrusive noises until Rowan became conscious only of the pounding of heartbeats and the hiss of a sharply-indrawn breath as Colt's mouth drew nearer, hovering over lips quivering soft and gentle as the wings of a butterfly—so easily crushed; so easily startled into panic-stricken flight.

'Rowan . . .!' he groaned in a torment of temptation. Then, displaying an uncertainty she had never before encountered in the man who had rampaged into her life, destroying her hopes, her solitude, and her peace of mind, he requested gently, 'Would you mind very much if I kissed you . . .?'

'I say, folks, they're here, our guests of honour have arrived!'

She jolted out of his arms when Abe's shout broke the spell that had almost seduced from her the shy, breathless denial for which Colt had been hoping. Closing her ears to a breathed curse consigning Abe to the fires of hell, she retreated like a startled fawn, backing straight into Abe, who was standing on the threshold, his wide grin slowly fading as he puzzled over the savage look flung his way by his obviously irate boss.

A concerted yell of welcome rose to the rafters when Colt appeared at her side and began leading his wildly blushing bride into the middle of the floor that had been swiftly cleared to accommodate a table covered with Kielder tartan on top of which had been placed a silver cake stand displaying a wedding cake iced and decorated with national symbols—the heather and thistle of Scotland entwined with English rosebuds.

Rowan fought hard to assume the attitude of cool composure expected of her position, but when Colt's hand enveloped hers, following the traditional custom of bride and bridegroom together cutting the first slice of wedding cake with a silver beribboned sword, she felt a treacherous wave of weakening, an urge to surrender to the strength emanating from a rock-hard arm holding her firmly against his side; from his tight, possessive grip upon her waist.

Her knowledge of tradition should have prepared her, the sea of smiling faces, the hands holding glasses aloft, preparing to toast the bride and groom, should have signalled a warning, but it was not until Colt's arm slid around her waist to draw her into a close embrace that she was reminded of the culminating act of ceremony.

All hell seemed to be set loose the moment his lips met hers, yells, whoops and cheers, the clashing of cymbals, the banging of drums, combined into a background of noise as shattering to her nerves as the baying of an advancing army. The impact of his kiss, thrusting as a blade into the heart of a rose, the crush of hands spanning her waist threatening to snap her lance-slim body in two, the intimate brush of lean cheeks and rough-velvet skin against her cheek, spearheaded an attack that routed all resistance, an oppressive, merciless, overpowering show of strength that forced her surrender and demonstrated her susceptibility to the devastating weapon of seduction she had never before encountered.

When finally, taking pity on her crushed mouth, Colt lifted his head to survey his victim with a gleam of triumph, her dazed blue eyes responded with a look of defeat that darkened to fear when Tom Graham's jubilant Celtic toast rang out above the babble of laughing, congratulatory voices.

> *'His plume is set with the holly green*
> *And the leaves of the rowan tree*
> *Lang life King Kielder!'*

Because pride demanded a show of composure, she acceded to the wishes of their chanting guests by allowing Colt to lead her on to the empty dance floor and nerved herself to submit to the torture of his possessive embrace while they waltzed to a tune played sweet, low and unashamedly romantic.

Her relief was tremendous when, after encircling the dance floor once, they were joined by a crush of eager dancers whose laughing exchanges made it possible for her to plead in an urgent undertone:

'Please, may we leave now?'

'Would any military tactician voluntarily retreat from a position of advantage?' he teased her gently, exploiting the need not to be overheard by resting his lips against the tender curve of her ear. 'If only I could believe that your request was prompted by an urge to enjoy my exclusive com-

pany! But as it is,' he shrugged regretfully, 'I feel
reluctant to release my captive bride whose re-
sponses are no less sweet because they're forced,
whose company I can claim at will, whom I can
kiss in front of wedding guests without fear of
having my face slapped.' He illustrated his point
by feathering his lips across her cheek and coolly
claiming her lips, prolonging the kiss until they
stood motionless, swaying in time to the music.
For lingering seconds Rowan felt she was floating
on air, then was jolted back to earth by a burst of
ribald laughter and an acute awareness of being
the object of dozens of laughing, sympathetic,
amused and envious eyes.

'Well, do you still want to leave?' He held her
ransom with a look that dared her to chance being
alone with him, leaving her no option but to fall
back on treachery as a ruse to escape from an intolerable situation.

'Yes, please . . .' She pretended a look of eager
longing, then as if overwhelmed by shyness she
cast down her lashes in a manner she guessed might
be typical of an enticing young bride. The
moment she heard his hissed-in breath, felt steel
hard muscles tensing against her spine, she knew
Colt had been fooled.

Suddenly she was released, left covered in
blushing confusion while he strode on to the platform and signalled the band to stop playing.

'Friends, colleagues, ladies and gentlemen!'
With the assurance of a redhaired giant he
addressed the gathering of guests. '. . . Regretfully, we must beg leave to be excused.

This has been a long though very enjoyable day and naturally my wife and I are feeling rather tired. Thank you for joining in our wedding celebrations, and I hope you'll stay so that the party can continue into the wee sma' hours of the morning.'

Cheers of appreciation followed his final wave and swift descent from the platform, then Rowan barely had time to register the swing of a kilt revealing a dirk stuck into the top of tartan hose, the purposeful advance of stury brogues, the sparkle of a jewelled brooch and the glint of silver buttons before she was plucked off her feet and into the arms of her reiver husband and swept, a bundle of furious feminine booty, towards the exit.

She could have screamed, yelled and ranted, just as many had done before her when threatened with abduction, but she hung on grimly to her dignity, even managed to cast her profile into a mould of serenity while she submitted to being lowered into the car and sitting without protest while Colt drove back to the castle.

A huge golden moon dipped and surfaced behind banked-up cloud so that one moment the fells were sharply outlined and the next obscured by shadows.

'A hunter's moon,' he indicated with a nod, displaying an uncanny ability to read her mind. 'The sort of night relished by steel-bonneted reivers who needed light to find a pathway through the bogs and shadows to cloak the dirtiest of deeds. It's a consolation to know that conflict is far behind us, Rowan,' he sounded deeply serious, 'good to be in a position to demonstrate to any remaining doubters that English and Scots make passionate foes—and equally passionate lovers.'

She could not trust herself to speak, but huddled into her wrap, using it as a shield to hide expressions of fear and uncertainty flitting across her expressive face. *Having No Remorse!* Her family motto sighed through her mind as if whispered by a vengeful spirit. *There is no shame in employing deeeit as a weapon against a deceiver, but tread cautiously, a step at a time, until you are out of the morass and can challenge Kielder strength from an unassailable position!*

The castle was deserted. As only the minimum number of rooms were in use—the rest bolted and left to gather dust—Nanny was the only live-in servant and she, for reasons of her own, had decided at the last minute to spend the night at her sister's house in the village once the party was over. So when they entered the hall Rowan shivered, sensitive to an ambience of threat, an aura of past conflict lingering within the castle that had contained many battles between English and Scots within its grim walls.

'Would you like a nightcap?' When Colt put a hand beneath her elbow to lead her towards the library she jerked out of reach.

'No, thank you,' she stammered, conscious of the need to keep a clear head, 'if you don't mind I'll go straight up to my . . . our . . . room.'

He smiled, eyeing her slim tenseness, her pale set features that looked sculpted from marble, with the resignation of a hunter used to the ways of timid creatures of the wild, a man who took time to stalk his prey and was prepared to be patient—for a little while longer.

'Rowan,' he closed the gap between them and captured her startled face between cupped hands, 'don't feel ashamed. Some defeats hold more triumph than victories. You displayed true bravery in acknowledging the futility of further conflict, so relax, brave heart, I promise you will not regret your surrender.'

The conceit of the man was unbelievable! She seethed behind the smiling mask she had donned in order to lull him into a mood of complacency.

'I'm sure I won't,' she agreed, quaking at the knees, reminding herself that coolness was imperative if she was to effect her escape. Trying to hide the cringing she felt when his hand stroked a tendril of hair from her cheek, she backed out of his clutches and started towards the stairs.

'You know where our rooms are situated?' she managed to choke across her shoulder.

'I do,' he called after her, a thread of laughter in his voice, 'I made it my business to find out!'

The suite of rooms Nanny had prepared in spite of orders to the contrary comprised a main bedroom panelled from ceiling to floor in dark, carved oak, dominated by a huge four-poster bed with drapes pulled back to reveal smooth plump pillows edged with lace, a heavy damask bedspread already turned down over paler green blankets and pristine sheets with one edge flicked back as if to offer comfort and encouragement to a shy bride, and a dressing-room and bathroom secreted behind two doors so symmetrically perfect they appeared as one with panelled walls.

Warmth from a fire burning low in a marble fireplace attracted her like a magnet, and she bathed in its glow as frantically she tossed her wedding-dress over her head, then, with a disgusted look at her best cotton nightdress laid out on the bed, rummaged through drawers and wardrobe in search of pyjamas and a serviceable dressing-gown to pull over her frozen limbs. Conscious that speed was the very essence of success, she did not wait to tidy her discarded clothes but ran towards a stretch of panelling, fumbled with an ornate piece of carving and gasped with relief when, with a slow, reluctant groan, a section slid open to reveal six stone steps leading up to a void of darkness. With the confidence of long practice she stepped through the aperture, heeled back the panelling, then struck a match taken from a box left on a ledge next to an ancient but serviceable oil lamp. Seconds later, with the lamp casting elongated shadows upon bare stone walls, she gained the safety of her hiding place, the secret room just large enough to accommodate a table, two chairs and a shelf full of books, that she and Nigel had considered their bolthole, a place used whenever they had felt the need to ponder in solitude, or to escape Nanny's wrath, during childhood.

For the first hour she tried to read, but gave up the effort when the strain of listening for sounds of movement in the room below made it impossible to concentrate. Then after she had sat for an age, staring blankly, cold began seeping into her bones, numbing until her flesh felt frozen, her limbs stiffly set, forcing her to acknowledge the foolishness of attempting to spend the rest of the long night entombed within an atmosphere chilly as an ice box.

She had entered a state of frozen paralysis, a trance-like immobility of mind and body brought about by stubbornness, a determination not to give an inch even if the outcome should be wilful self-destruction, when a sound impinged upon her subconscious—the creaking of ancient woodwork, perhaps, or the squeaking of a mouse—but she was too miserable to care.

'Have you suffered enough, or shall I leave you to indulge in masochistic penance for a while longer?'

She raised her head from forearms stretched out across the table to direct a stupefied stare at the angry figure with fists thrust savagely into the pockets of a dressing-gown, glowering from the doorway.

'How . . . how did you know where to find me?' she husked, swallowing painfully.

'How could an adventurous schoolboy, his curiosity fired by servants' gossip, fail to discover a priest's hole whose location is common knowledge?'

'You mean . . .' she struggled to sit upright, wincing from the suspicion that her agony had been unnecessary, 'that you've known all along that I was here? Then why . . .?' She stopped abruptly, wondering why the thought of his indifference should cause her extra pain.

'Because you deserved to be taught a lesson,' he told her tightly, 'and because nothing I could have done would have inflicted more misery than you've inflicted upon yourself!' In two strides he reached her side. Lowering his head until she felt drowned by the upheaval in grey, storm-tossed eyes, he charged thickly: 'No doubt you thought you had me fooled, but in spite of my optimistic claim that we could achieve an amicable partnership, I felt your capitulation was too sudden to be completely believable. You see, Rowan, I can't help being aware of the depth of animosity you feel towards me—even so, until tonight I hadn't suspected that your hatred ran so deep you would choose to freeze to death rather than accept me as a husband!'

She moaned a protest when he stooped to lift her into his arms, but was too chilled to put up much of a fight when he carried her downstairs and into a bedroom glowing with the warmth of a stoked-up fire. The spitting of logs, the roar of flames leaping up the chimney sounded no less furious than the threat smouldered against her ear as, tightening his grip upon her numbed body, Colt directed her attention towards the moon sailing past an uncurtained window.

'A hunter's moon, Rowan, remember . . .? A moon reivers looked upon as an omen of success whenever they felt the urge to ride, rape, pillage and plunder!'

CHAPTER SEVEN

ONCE again Falstone Castle had been taken by storm, this time by an army of builders who had erected scaffolding in the downstairs rooms and were in the process of carrying out Colt's orders to replace rotting timbers, renew outdated plumbing, and discover the source of damp rising and seeping in dark patches through damask-covered walls. Every room in the castle was to be renovated, even those that had been locked and left deserted for decades, before a second wave of workers descended, experts in the art of restoring the interiors of ancient buildings to their former glory.

It had taken the dynamic new owner of Falstone less than a week to set the ball rolling, yet Rowan felt, as she sat in the breakfast room toying with a piece of toast and sipping coffee, that the banging of hammers and the rasping of saws through wood had been assaulting her ears for an eternity. Surprisingly, Nanny had proffered no complaints about the upheaval. Indeed, she sounded aggravatingly cheerful when she appeared with a tray to clear the dishes from the table.

'You'll be staying in this morning?' Suspiciously, she eyed the baggy jumper and disreputable denims which Rowan, almost as a defence mechanism, had adopted as a uniform.

'I have to ride over to the cottages.' She tensed, anticipating an argument. 'Old Mrs Story has sent word that she wants to see me urgently.'

'To ask the chiropodist to tend to her corns, no doubt!' Nanny snorted. 'Ann Story was a fusser in her teens and has grown worse with old age. You must make it known that you're far too busy to be at the beck and call of everyone.' She banged the tray down on the table, to the detriment of an ancient coffee pot. 'We're taking on extra household staff and Mr Kielder has arranged for you to interview some people from the village this morning.'

'Then he ought to have had the courtesy to tell me first!' Rowan jumped to her feet, her blue eyes flashing.

'You're quite right,' a voice drawled from the doorway. 'I'm sorry, the interviews slipped my mind. Immediately I remembered, I left the site hoping to tell you in person, but obviously,' he grimaced, sauntering into the room, 'Nanny has beaten me to it.'

Displaying a deference Rowan found galling, Nanny almost bobbed a curtsey before retreating from an atmosphere reeking with acrimony.

It had been raining heavily all morning, but Colt seemed impervious to damp that had toned his hair to a deep, rich chestnut red, or to rivulets of moisture coursing slowly down a hard jawline and a length of bronzed neck, then left glistening on a hairy chest left exposed to the elements by a partly unbuttoned shirt and a sheepskin jacket he had shrugged over broad shoulders and then left casually undone.

Startled by an impulse to berate him for a careless disregard for his own well-being, she edged nervously towards the window, hoping to conceal a blush from grey eyes used to scanning far horizons, pinpointing and assessing every movement, every slight area of activity.

'I'm afraid you'll have to carry out the interviews yourself,' she told him stiffly. 'I have a previous engagement.'

'Then break it.' She tensed, sensing his approach from the rear, and reacted as to the stab of a rapier when his hand clamped down upon her shoulder, spinning her round to face him.

'*Don't touch me!*' She jerked away, shocked by an attack of sharply-needled nerves. Hating his easy dominance, his ability to arouse her emotions in spite of a strong will to remain calm, she refused coldly. 'Unlike yourself, once a promise has been given I never go back on my word.'

'Don't you, Rowan . . .?' The cynical question hovered over her head, making her want to cower, timid as a mouse under threat from a bird of prey. She braced to combat the humiliation of being reminded of her marriage vows . . . to *love, honour, and obey . . . with this body I thee worship*. On that count, at least, he had little room for complaint!

Then for some reason his keen glance softened as it roved a suddenly wounded mouth that refused to be still, and he decided to be kind.

'Part of our bargain was that you would relieve me of all household responsibilities,' he reminded her quietly, 'to make this a place where I could come home to and relax.'

She was ashamed of feeling so ridiculously grateful for his compassion in throwing her a lifeline when he could have decimated her pride at a stroke.

'The surroundings are hardly conducive to relaxation,' she pointed out, her heart keeping pace with the furious pounding of hammers.

'Point taken,' he agreed wryly, when the air was rent by the high-pitched whine of an electric drill, 'but to a man who has known only transient shelter, the essence of a home lies in its permanence—a house at journey's end that is familiar, where he'll find a wife to humour his moods; servants to minister to his comfort, and children,' he concluded meaningfully, 'to set the final seal upon his happiness.'

This hint of his intentions revived a painful memory, provoking the blush that was never far from her cheeks, a lingering, scorching momento of a night she would have preferred to forget. Unable to withstand his steady scrutiny, she turned her face aside.

'I suppose I could delay my business until after lunch,' she conceded with difficulty, wondering why, in spite of her determination to oppose him at every turn, she should find herself continually bending to his will.

'Thank you, Rowan . . .' the warmth of his tone sent a tremor running up her spine, 'from past experience I knew that I could depend upon you to be . . . generous.'

When the door closed quietly behind him she

slumped down on to the windowseat and gave way
to the relief of tears, a tempest of contradictory
emotions made up of shame and pride, fear and
elation, misery and passionate, demoralising, un-
educated pleasure. More than a week had past
since the night she had been dragged back in time
to the days of plundering reivers and had lived
out the trauma of a girl abducted by an enemy
motivated by anger, resentment of defeat, and a
desire to see the pride of a ruling English family
trampled underfoot by forcing physical union
upon a youthful maiden in the hope that hated
Scottish seed might flourish and grow fruitful in
fertile, virgin soil, yet every moment of every
passing day she felt conscious of being humbled,
in the way a soldier is humbled when he loses a
battle and is then condemned by his enemy to the
ranks of walking wounded.

Clasped within angry arms, with his fiery
breath fanning her cheek, and the pulsating heat
of his hard masculine body crushing her into a
nest of downy blankets, the blood had quickly
melted in her frozen veins, beginning as a tingling trickle, then a surge, and finally developing
into a racing torrent of new and frightening
feeling. She had fought as her predecessors must
have fought, with raking fingernails, snapping
teeth and wildly flailing limbs, yet she had
sensed from his indulgent growl of laughter that
he was enjoying restraining her puny efforts.
Feinting blows from her clenched fists, he had
pinned her kicking legs with the weight of his
body and imprisoned her wrists in a steely grip,

stretching her arms out wide until the only defence left to her had been an angry tongue and
contemptuously blazing eyes.

Then all at once he had seemed to tire of the
skirmish and had silenced her tirade with a kiss
more stunning than a blow, forceful as the waters
of a dam that had seemed gradually to build up
inside her before bursting with a thunderous roar,
spilling an overflow of passion that had mingled
with his to form a racing, boiling, pounding current that had tossed them together in a maelstrom
of ecstasy before disgorging their shaking, clinging, exhausted bodies into calmer, less turbulent
waters.

He had been kind in victory, rough wooing had
given way to gentle consideration, to whispered
assurances mingling with kisses pressed without
ceasing upon her trembling, responsive lips, and
with a soothing, sensitive touch of hands that had
caressed her into contented stillness so that for a
while they had slept with naked limbs entwined,
half-drowned castaways tossed on to a peaceful
shore, until the dam had filled once more to
danger level, floodgates had burst open, and with
joyful confidence they had welcomed a second
vortex of rapturous emotion.

'Rowan, my love,' Colt had charged in a shaken
groan, 'you have the sweet, pure breath of a child,
the candid generosity of the very young—and the
sensuous allure of a she-devil!'

But the mysteries of womanhood, her illogical,
feminine reaction to overwhelming emotion had
proved him to be unversed in the ways of

women—her kind of woman—for once the storm had abated leaving them calm she had sought relief from unbearable tension by bursting into tears. He had held her loosely, wincing from the scorch of tears upon a muscled chest toughened and bronzed from exposure to the elements, then had shocked her into silence with an oath ripped savagely from a constricted throat.

'Dammit, Rowan, did you have to cry!'

Seconds later she had been left alone, staring dry-eyed through the window at a hunter's moon sailing high in the heavens, wondering if others had felt as shamed, bewildered, and bereft when abandoned by a passionate enemy.

The interviewing of applications eager to fill the posts of gardeners, kitchen helpers and general cleaners did not take long. The villagers were all well known to her, so it was simply a matter of agreeing suitable hours and rates of pay before she was free to saddle up Cello and set off to keep her appointment.

She rode at a leisurely pace, enjoying the sight of miles of wild moorland—marshy ground growing only rank grass providing rough pasturage for a few sheep—spruce-covered hills breaking up the smooth outline of the moors, and acres of conifer forest, a soft flowing monotone of dark blue-green broken by occasional patches of brighter green larch.

Avoiding high ridges that looked down upon the scarred valley, she headed Cello into the forest in search of solitude, hoping to erase some of the jumpy tension that had plagued her for days. But

a glimpse of the little church in the forest sen-
tinelled by shapely Irish yews set her pulses
aching with a reminder of her wedding day, so
that not even the discovery that the inhabitants of
the forest were still grazing unconcerned by the
daily encroaching noise of machinery was suffici-
ently comforting to curb tremors of nervous tension.

Consequently, she was all the more alarmed, all
the more ready to erupt into anger, when deep
inside the forest she picked up the sound of a
tuneless whistle as she neared a clearing and saw
the figure of a man squatting low over a bulging
haversack.

'Why are you here?'

Abe spun round, startled by the pistol-sharp
question, then immediately relaxed with an expression of relief.

'Lady Rowan,' he grinned, 'you gave me one
hell of a . . . you scared the daylight out of me,'
he amended hastily.

She was in no mood for banter. Fastening eyes
hard with suspicion upon the haversack at his feet,
she demanded icily: 'I insist upon knowing why
you're here!'

'For a very innocuous reason, I assure you.' He
forked his fingers through his hair in a gesture of
bewilderment. 'I was merely intending to record
some bird calls—it's a hobby of mine.' He halted,
made awkward by her unfriendly attitude. 'I ear-
marked this spot weeks ago because of its lack of
background noise and seeming isolation. As you
can see,' he flipped open the cover of his haver-

sack with his foot, 'I have with me a tape recorder and microphone—I trust you have no objection?'

Rowan slipped out of the saddle to examine thoroughly the contents of the haversack.

'Don't you believe me?' Abe sounded indignant, and slightly hurt. 'What were you expecting to find in there, a couple of snares?'

She straightened. 'I'm sorry, Mr . . . Abe,' she tendered a strained smile, 'if I appear unduly suspicious. Unfortunately, we've found it necessary over the years to keep a close watch upon known habitats of protected species of birds, nevertheless, in spite of our vigilance and what some might consider to be an unnecessary amount of secrecy, word has spread and many precious eggs have been stolen from nests by thoughtless amateur collectors.'

'Blast their selfish hides!' His spontaneous outburst of disgust forged an immediate affinity. Rowan relaxed, reassured by the ferocity of his frown, then by way of an apology for suspecting him of such sacrilege, she proffered an olive branch.

'There's another reason why the protection of this clearing is so vital,' she confided, leading him towards a spot beneath the trees where the ground was thick with moss and rotted pine needles. She knelt down and carefully cleared a small area of vegetation, then sat back upon her heels, inviting him to take a look.

He puzzled over what looked to him no more than a dead main stem that had various side branches with a just-visible growth of new shoots branching either side of it.

'It's an orchid—one of a nest of rare orchids known as Creeping Lady's Tresses that appear only in a few scattered locations where the habitat is suitable. You must come back and see it in July when the blooms are at their best—creamy white, short and plump, with a heavenly scent that attracts every pollinating bumble bee for miles around.' His expression reflected recognition of the honour she had paid him and when she had carefully re-covered her secret store and walked back to the clearing, he found words to express his gratitude.

'Thank you for allowing me to share your secret, Lady Rowan—for allowing me to become a member of what I guess must be a very tight circle of confidants.'

'Only two other people besides myself know about the orchids,' she confirmed. 'You must promise me, Abe, that you will never, under any circumstances, betray my trust by telling anyone else of their existence?'

'Cut my throat and hope to die!' Solemnly, he wetted a finger and traced a line across his neck from ear to ear. 'Everyone back at camp treats me like an irresponsible boy—especially Colt—yet you, who can't be much older than myself, didn't hesitate to entrust me with knowledge kept even from local inhabitants. I promise you'll never have cause to regret it,' he assured her, his usually devil-may-care expression replaced by a depth of earnestness. 'And in return,' he hesitated, blushing to the roots of his hair, 'might I extract from you a promise not to mention my . . . er . . . hobby to any of my workmates? They're a tough bunch of guys,' he explained with obvious embarrassment, 'with hearts of gold, each and every one of them, but their interest in birds is strictly confined to the young female variety.'

'Commonly known as chicks . . .?' She smiled, sympathetic to his need to keep secret a hobby that might give rise to derisive comment and detract from his macho image. 'Of course you have my promise, but I feel certain you're being unduly sensitive; every wildcat, however ferocious, has a small grain of tabby in his composition.'

'Then all I can say is that, in the case of my buddies, they keep it very well hidden,' Abe countered gloomily.

'Even Colt . . .?' She wished she could speak his name without a catch in her voice.

'Especially Colt.' He was bending to retrieve his haversack so did not notice her wince. 'Any hopes we might have harboured about marriage mellowing his temper have been dispelled this past week—only yesterday he tore a strip off a guy who dubbed him King Kielder within earshot, even though he must be aware by now that the nickname has well and truly stuck.' When he turned round to face her, with a thermos in one hand and a packet of sandwiches in the other, the tight set of her features must have communicated displeasure. 'Heck, have I spoken out of turn again? And just as I was about to ask you to share my lunch!'

He looked so downcast she felt forced to relent.

'What a lovely idea, it's ages since I enjoyed a meal *al fresco*.'

As they sat on a fallen treetrunk demolishing with relish generous helpings of ham sandwiched between slices of bread baked early that morning in the camp cookhouse, washed down with coffee made memorable by a rich aroma rising in the air to mingle with the scent of resin, Rowan felt tension seeping out of her, could almost have convinced herself that the clock had been turned back to the peaceful era she had enjoyed before the invasion, had it not been for a faint sound in the background like the rumble of distant artillery, indicating the presence of an army bent upon destruction.

Time sped on wings as they chatted amicably, discovering more and more areas of mutual interest, establishing a rapport that dispersed Abe's awe of her elevated position and helped her to recognise him as a kindred spirit, youthful, willing to undertake responsibilities, yet basically uncertain.

Which probably accounted for the ease with which, in response to her enquiry about his job, he displayed irritation.

'I'll always be grateful to Colt for taking me on his payroll, but after five years you'd imagine he'd stop treating me as a probationer, show me a little trust, so that I could prove my worth and dispel the reminder that initially he took me on only as a favour to my sister.'

'Your sister?' she prompted, conscious of a sudden return of tension.

'Diane,' he enlightened moodily, completely absorbed in his own misery. 'She's a fashion model—working in London at the moment—but when she first met up with Colt she was just an amateur striving to achieve recognition in the States. His influence helped to get her career off the ground. But as ever since the death of our parents she's reacted towards me like a broody hen, Colt relieved her of all responsibility by offering me a post designed to provide me with a promising future.'

In spite of her revulsion, her contempt of self-inflicted pain, she forced herself to probe further.

'Colt and your sister must have been very close?'

'They were,' he nodded, unknowingly twisting a knife in her wound, 'but Diane was never under any illusion about having a special place in his affections. I realised that she was content to be one of many, when she confided: "*Colt always needs a mountain to climb. Whenever a peak has been conquered he's content for a while, but then he becomes bored and has to lift his sights higher.*" '

Rowan shrank from the matter-of-fact statement that confirmed what she had suspected—that to Colt Kielder she represented no more than a challenge, a rare and distant peak that had to be scaled to be reduced to the ordinary. He possessed the vital attraction of power most women found irresistible, power of physique and power of achievement, yet even he, accustomed though he must have become to quick conquests, must have been surprised at the ease with which his latest target had been accomplished!

Dusk had fallen by the time she had concluded her business and returned to the castle. Without bothering to change, she made her way to the dining-room where she knew Colt would be waiting to begin his evening meal, and as she walked across a darkened hall, its walls lined with scaffolding, she felt a sense of imprisonment, a feeling of being trapped within a state of siege.

'Where the devil have you been?' He whipped around from the window, his expression clamped as a man who has kept close vigil. 'I'd begun to wonder if you'd been thrown, if Cello had perhaps stumbled?'

'It's been such a lovely day, I lost all track of time.' Rowan tried to sound airy as she prepared to take her seat at the table, but regretted her show of bravado when his hand fastened upon her shoulder, then froze, as if fighting an impulse to shake her.

'Have you so little concern for those who worry about your welfare? You were absent so long that even Nanny had begun to panic—and just look at you!' His disgusted glance raked from the crown of her dishevelled head to the soles of mud-caked boots. 'How much longer do you intend keeping up an act of childish defiance, parading the most disreputable garments in your wardrobe in order to try my patience?'

'I've always lived too far removed from society to bother about feeding my vanity with fashion!' she retorted, daring to cast a scornful eye over an impeccable white shirt, silk Hermès tie, and a black velvet dinner jacket stroking cat-supple over muscular shoulders. 'Anyway,' she chanced the utmost show of temerity, 'it's a mistake to appear too well dressed when aspiring to being accepted by the aristocracy! According to my brother, who's something of an expert on clothes, the "preppy" look is now all the rage in London— identical sporty T-shirts, trousers, striped blazers and jackets being worn by both sexes. Therefore it's arguable,' she challenged triumphantly, twirling a full circle in order to display her boyish outfit to full advantage, 'that what I'm wearing is socially unacceptable!'

Her attack ought to have totally destroyed his vanity, but there was no hint of blight in eyes narrowed with annoyance, no honed edge to the voice that rasped sharp as a saw through wood:

'You resemble a popular song that's been sung too often, a melody redolent of stables, manure, and sweaty horse blankets! But as I'm paying the piper I intend choosing both the tune *and* the composer. I have a friend whose exquisite taste and eye for colour has made her internationally famous in the fashion world—I'll telephone her tonight and test her ability to choose a wardrobe with no more than a description and a set of measurements to give clues to the intended wearer.'

Obviously, he was referring to Diane! The compliment to his one-time mistress made her resentment soar.

'You can't supply my measurements, even I don't know what they are because I've never bothered to take them,' she told him stiffly.

'The solution to that problem lies as near as a tape measure,' he clipped. A shaft of light beamed down upon his lowering head, firing his hair torch-bright as he stressed with a menacing glitter: 'I should search one out, if I were you, little warrior, for should the information I require not be forthcoming I may feel forced to resort to Braille!'

CHAPTER EIGHT

THE contents of the castle supplied a record of the history of past inhabitants, a study of their lifestyle that began with a few odd items of primitive, purely functional furniture that had survived the ravages of sixteenth-century warfare then continued to demonstrate, by way of carpets, needlework, wrought iron and ormolu mounts, clocks and furniture, the developing style and taste of a procession of Falstone earls.

When Nigel sold his birthright the entire contents of the castle had been included in the deal, and as Rowan supervised the removal and storage of objects in danger of being damaged if left in the vicinity of workmen, she was struck by the bitter thought that although civilisation might have advanced, the attitude of one man in particular was attuned to that of the Dark Ages when it had been common practice to barter for a wife in the marketplace.

Rooms left uninhabited for years had been utilised for the storage of irreplaceable items, and as she traced a finger through dust covering a black marble top inset with a fantastic variety of various-coloured marbles and semi-precious stones depicting leaves, flowers and birds, Rowan became suddenly still, her senses alerted by the ring of footsteps crossing the stone paved hall.

Only one man of her acquaintance strode impatient as a god of war thirsting for battle!

'So this is where you've hidden yourself!' Colt towered in the doorway, grey eyes quizzing her slender, dejected figure, a pensive mouth, and drooping, raven-black head. 'What are you doing?' He advanced into the room, treading wary as a cat towards a shrinking bird.

'Taking inventory of your assets, as requested,' she replied, then added sarcastically: 'I've listed myself under items of Swag.'

When grey eyes clouded she realised that she had made the foolish mistake of underestimating the intelligence of an adversary.

'There's no denying your classical perfection,' he agreed dryly, 'yet you're hardly petrified enough to be likened to a carved garland of foliage—more of an Amorine, perhaps . . .?'

She blushed when his lips tugged upward in a smile, conscious that his mind was dwelling upon their wedding night, the night he had asserted his right to caress her naked-Cupid form, to love like a lion—before spurning naïveté as boring. This train of thought seemed confirmed when his glance fell upon a delicately sculptured torchère depicting chained Nubian slaves holding aloft glass lampshades moulded into the shape of flaming torches, an extravagant vulgarity purchased by one of the more flamboyant earls of Falstone.

'Petrified poetry,' he murmured, and somehow she knew that he was not referring to the shapely nudes immortalised in marble. 'Nature recognises no indecencies, yet man is bludgeoned into following laws of decorum, ceremony, and manners that decree he must do this, or he must not do that. Is it so unforgivable, Rowan,' he turned on her so fiercely she stepped back alarmed, 'for a man to fall victim to the promptings of his own nature? Is propriety really so important to a woman that she's unable to forgive a man who made her blush?'

'Sovereigns seldom seek forgiveness,' she reminded him stiffly, 'their consciences are usually salved by declaring an amnesty, an act by which kings can pardon injustices committed by themselves!' With fingernails digging deeply into her palms, she steeled herself not to read penitence in a face grown suddenly sombre, not to be deceived into thinking that his stern mouth could ever be softened by remorse.

He was near enough to touch her, close enough for passionate vibrations to breach the chasm between them so that inward quivering forced her to back away until the edge of a nearby table lent support to her trembling limbs. The distant sound of hammering merged with her heartbeats until her ears felt deafened by the din, her body rendered inert by pulses that leapt into throbbing life immediately he drew nearer.

But the threat to her shaky defences was averted when after an angry bombardment of her pale, pinched face, Colt thrust clenched fists deep into the pockets of his jacket and bit savagely:

'If that's how our marriage appears to you—an act of injustice—how do you see yourself? As a wife sacrificed on the altar of duty?'

For one wildly illogical moment she felt tempted to absolve him of guilt with a denial, by confessing that she had emerged from the sacrificial rite revitalised, with senses more acute, nerves vibrant and tingling, with a body that had been permitted a taste of paradise and left with a gnawing hunger for more. She stabbed back the impulse, but the shock of knowing herself capable of such traitorous thoughts startled her blue eyes wide with self-accusation.

'How do you expect me to feel?' Her forced whisper seemed to hover like smoke over his damped-down furnace of wrath. 'I've been bought, wedded, and bedded, but you won't break my pride; her chin tilted high as Falstone courage, 'whatever further punishment you might impose, I will not be consumed by your insatiable appetite for power!'

'So, you are to be a morsel forever sticking in my throat, hoping, no doubt, that some day I might choke,' he drawled, looking suddenly dangerous. 'But what if I should grow tired of the indigestible and decide to spit it out?'

'I'd prefer to be a crumb in the belly of a sparrow,' she indicted coldly, 'than allow a beast to gorge upon my carcase.'

The convulsive jerk of hands thrust deep into his pockets should have signalled an elated sense of victory, but though for once her dice had thrown up a winning score, misery smothered every faint flicker of satisfaction. It seemed hard to believe that Colt's tough, rawhide skin had developed a sensitive spot, yet after seconds of strained silence his voice when he spoke sounded flat, his shrug seemed defeated.

'I sought you out this morning in order to broach an idea I thought might meet with your approval.' His swift change of subject took her by surprise. When he stooped to examine a cabinet panelled with oyster veneering radiating circles of end cuts of wood displaying the natural growth rings of the tree, his expression became hidden. 'As every generation seems to have left its cultural mark upon the castle, I wondered if you might like to perpetuate the custom by decorating one of the rooms entirely to your own taste, using your own choice of fittings and furniture. It's been said that a person's choice of surroundings can be considered a reflection of hidden character,' he straightened to direct a brief, noncommittal smile, 'so it would be a shame, don't you think, if posterity were to be denied the closing chapter of Falstone family history?'

'Before the advent of King Kielder . . .?' Rowan almost sneered, incensed by his peremptory dismissal of her proud family line. 'No doubt your reign will herald a quest for luxury in terms of comfort, an entire devotion to the type of splendour deemed a necessary status symbol by the newly-rich. Are you planning to have Gucci dogs in every alcove, a diamond-studded doorbell, and gold-plated toothpicks on the dining table? Or would you prefer a mink-lined Jacuzzi in the bathroom?'

Like a bear prodded beyond endurance, Colt rounded with a snarl to clutch her shoulders between hands powerful enough to crush.

'What I would prefer above all else, Rowan, is a truce, an intermission, a respite from constant sparring. Even warring barons of the Dark Ages agreed to stop carving each other up, burning each other's wheatfields, raping each other's women—at least on Sundays, feast days, and church holy days! I would be grateful if just once I could waken knowing that for one day at least I'll be granted a small truce, one that begins at daybreak and continues peacefully through until sundown. Must it remain a pipe dream, Rowan?' he shook her fiercely. 'I've tried as hard as I know how to atone for my mistakes, to merit some sign of approval—is your purse of pardon so tight that even the small gift of leniency is more than you can afford?'

Before words had time to form on her startled lips he had gone—flung out of the room in a temper of frustration!

Miserably, she forced herself to continue with her task of taking inventory of oak chairs with carved lions displaying the rose of England; a lacquered cabinet on a silvered stand; a gaming table and matching stool; an oak sofa plushly upholstered in pink; a round satinwood table; an ornate cabinet veneered with tortoiseshell; giltwood mirrors; elegant clocks with fine ormolu mounts; a pair of Regency armchairs covered with olive green velvet; a walnut stool with needleworked seat—all allegedly prizes of war taken by successive earls of Falstone, uniquely valuable items that Nigel had attempted to sell, only to discover that because of torn upholstery, chipped woodwork, cracked glass and missing handles, their value had been considerably reduced.

She blessed her forebears whose careless attitude had ensured she would not be deprived of familiar objects she had grown to love, but as she moved among relics of a more glorious past her mind was concentrated upon the present, and more exactly upon the husband who had taken her as a prize of war with the sole object of revenge against the hated English aristocracy. It seemed that now he had achieved his aim he wanted hostilities to cease, so far as he was concerned the war was over—so far as she was concerned it had only just begun!

She was still pondering over his dislike of her family, and especially of her brother Nigel, when Nanny entered the room.

'Kielder's gone.' She had adopted this form of address for the master of the house, pronouncing his surname with the sort of deference usually accorded to a title. 'What have you said to make him go storming out of the castle with a brow as black as thunder?'

'Or a child in a tantrum because he can't get his own way?' Rowan qualified coolly.

'Some child!' Nanny snorted, breaking into a chuckle as grating as the hinges on a long-unopened door. 'He was born big as a toddler; at three he looked old enough for school, and at twelve he was already showing signs of developing into a tall, broad-shouldered man.'

'You watched him growing up, then?' Rowan

bit her lip, hoping Nanny had not read her note of eager surprise.

'But of course I did—and his father before him!' she retorted with a pride usually reserved for her own kith and kin. 'Even when impoverished, the Kielders are not the sort of men who can be overlooked—indeed, among Scottish Borderers they've always been as highly revered as Falstones are by the English. Surely you must recall playing with him when you were a child?' Nanny shot her a surprised glance. 'During the school holidays he came every day to the castle and was allowed to run loose in the grounds until his mother had finished her work.'

Rowan's brow wrinkled as she concentrated hard, trying to revive memories of the distant past. With the master of the household seldom in residence discipline had grown lax, so that many of the children whose fathers worked on the estate had regarded the paths winding through overgrown shrubberies, the neglected orchards, the deserted outhouses and stables, as a huge adventure playground.

'There was one boy,' she began diffidently, then with growing conviction, 'whose red head always towered above the rest—he was always bullying Nigel!'

'That would be Kielder,' Nanny nodded, looking suddenly shamefaced, 'but though your brother always insisted that he was being bullied, I often suspected that the boot was actually on the other foot, because in spite of his superior physique, Kielder was noted for his protective manner towards those less robust than himself, especially the little ones. Whereas your brother, I'm afraid to say,' her thin lips pursed, 'was always inclined to take advantage of his position.'

'He did throw his weight about rather,' Rowan felt forced to agree.

'We'll never know the true ins and outs of the affair,' Nanny continued to brood, 'but after one final scrape involving all three of you, Kielder was banned from entering the castle grounds ever again. You and he were discovered all muddy and soaking wet and Nigel covered in bruises and with a black eye.'

Rowan sat down suddenly when out of the depths of her subconscious shot a startling spear of recall. She had been less than five years old at the time, yet the experience had left her with a horror of dark, dank tunnels. During one of many forays of exploration that had been a favourite childhood pursuit, some of the older children had stumbled across an old, dried-up well. Years before, its head had been sealed with planks nailed across its rim, but rotted timber had yielded to the probing of a dozen pairs of hands that had uncovered a black void deep enough to encourage the childish fantasy that it was a bottomless pit, an endless tunnel boring straight through the planet.

Arguments had ensued about the advisability of testing the strength of the length of rope still coiled around an overhead beam that had once been used with a bucket attached to draw water from the well. Rowan remembered clearly that it had been Nigel, who had always taken charge whenever the redhaired boy was absent, who had insisted that she, being the smallest and lightest of them all, should be lowered down the well in order to prove his assertion that it was shallow, merely the depth of the length of rope. Even while mulling over the incident beads of sweat chilled her brow as she experienced in retrospect the trauma of being tied with rope beneath her armpits, then lowered, kicking and screaming in protest, into what had appeared to her childish mind as a black hole of eternity. Then her terrified scream when the knot had come undone, dropping her swift as a stone into a bed of evil-smelling mud.

The events that had followed had merged into a panic-stricken blur. She knew she had screamed and pleaded hysterically with faces ringed around a patch of daylight high above her head to come down and fetch her. She remembered Nigel's shaken, very frightened voice urging her not to panic as he was going to fetch help, then there had followed the sound of argument, a scuffle, and a yell of pain from Nigel, before the small spot of daylight had disappeared as a body had begun lowering down the rope towards her.

She knew now that it had been Colt who had encouraged her not to be afraid while he had tied the rope competently beneath her armpits, that it had been his voice that had urged her to remain calm while jerkily, laboriously, she had been hauled towards the surface. Which method he had used to climb out of the well she had never dis-

covered, because from that day onwards he had
been banished from the castle grounds, banned
from approaching within yards of the son of the
Earl of Falstone, who must have sworn to Nanny
and to every other adult concerned that he was
blameless, that the villain of the piece was one of
the distrusted Scots, son of the hothead Kielder.

*Was it any wonder Colt held a hard contempt for
English justice—that for years he had bided his time,
determined to wreak revenge upon both deceitful
Falstones!*

An hour later, in spite of the fact that a grey
veil of mist was wreathing the fells and a steady
drizzle of rain borne upon high winds was soaking
sheep huddled for protection against drystone
walls and turning trickling burns into chocolate-
coloured froth racing down fellsides to disgorge
into an already swollen river, she set out to keep
what had become a regular tryst with Abe.

He had one whole day off each week, and without prior arrangement, without so much as a hint
of verbal collusion, they had formed the habit of
making their way to the clearing where the first
seeds of friendship had been sown. He was awaiting her arrival with a broad grin of welcome that
erupted immediately he heard the thud of Cello's
hoofbeats.

'I must try to hire a mount,' he confided ruefully, as he helped her down from the saddle. 'I've
left my car bogged down in mud at the edge of the
forest—some parts of the road are so badly flooded
I thought I wasn't going to make it! Doesn't it
ever do anything else but rain around here?'

'Presumably, the amount of rainfall was one of the deciding factors in the choice of location for the dam,' she reminded him dryly. 'We do get a lot of rain and snow and high winds, but as always, there are compensations, for when the sun begins glowing through the mist, throwing a mantle of red-gold bracken over the sloping shoulders of fells, when every leaf and blade glistens tear-bright, and the air is filled with the twittering and fluttering of birds drying off their feathers, the countryside seems newly-born, fresh, clean and sweet-smelling.'

'That's how I always think of you.' The words seemed jerked from his lips without volition. For a second he looked startled by his own temerity, but when she smiled, accepting the compliment as it had been meant—a genuine, non-flirtatious expression of admiration—he smiled his relief.

'D'you know what I admire most about the girls in this region,' he confided as they left Cello to graze and began sauntering along the path through the forest, 'their lack of coquetry, their acceptance that a guy, in spite of being a member of the opposite sex, is capable of friendship. Take Dale, for instance—I don't think I've ever felt so relaxed, so uncommitted to the chore of searching my mind for compliments, in the company of any other girl—with the exception of yourself.'

'Who was it that said, "a compliment is akin to a kiss through a veil, a compromise between giving a woman what is forbidden and denying her what is her due"?' Rowan mused. 'Personally,' she had no idea how sad she suddenly sounded, 'I think the greatest compliment a man can pay to a woman is honesty.'

'Then you must be pleased you married Colt,' Abe decided cheerfully, unaware that the very mention of his name had caused her to flinch, 'for he is the one contradiction I know of to the theory that an honest man is a man condemned to poverty. To some of his more recent recruits, men who haven't worked with him long enough to know him well, he sometimes appears aloof and none too approachable, rather tight-lipped about bad language and dirty jokes—imposing no bans, you understand, just making culprits feel definitely uneasy—yet even so he communicates such integrity, such a sense of justice and fair play, that every one of them, from the rawest to the toughest, is soon committed to following him to hell. Even in the boardroom where his contempt of needless courtesy, his reputation for aiming straight for the jugular, offends many who enjoy the ritual ceremonies of business deals, his friendship is prized, his character and ability so respected that directors are prepared to accept his crucial sums scribbled on the back of an envelope, before the findings of expert accountants.'

'I've no need to be convinced that my husband is a man of action,' she rebuked a trifle bitterly. 'I know only too well how he thrives upon dealing and manipulating, upon imposing his will on others. Of course he's a driving force, but heading where . . .? Only he knows.'

'So you, too, have spotted his one weakness.' When he pulled her to a halt she saw that his brow was furrowed into lines of anxiety. 'Colt rarely stops working because he seems to find it impossible to delegate responsibility. The fact that I have a personal axe to grind is immaterial, management structure is so sparse he's stretched tight as an elastic band trying to keep tabs on everything. Even his social life has tended in the past to be restricted to dinner parties with top executives, and they more often than not have evolved from social chit-chat into a business discussion. We all expected—hoped—that marriage would put an end to his bad working habits, but it simply hasn't happened, he's still pushing himself too hard, almost as if,' he hesitated, reluctant to give offence, then forced the grim conclusion, 'he were a compulsive gambler risking his all in the hope of hitting some elusive jackpot.'

In spite of her conviction that he was worrying needlessly about a human dynamo whose ego thrived upon power, Rowan felt shamed by the slight hint of criticism lurking among his words.

'I'm sorry if my conduct has fallen short of the standards expected of the wife of your boss,' she replied stiffly, 'but as you and your colleagues must know, my husband is a law unto himself and is therefore hardly likely to allow me to influence the habits of a lifetime.'

But the imperious rebuke, far from having the effect she had intended, surprised from him a hoot of laughter.

'My dear Lady Rowan, if you can't persuade him to relax no one can!'

She found his teasing grin infuriating. 'Why

me?' She all but stamped her foot. 'Why should I be singled out to exert pressure upon my husband?'

His grin slowly faded as he sensed bewilderment mixed with fiery indignation. 'Because,' he spelled out slowly and distinctly, as if anxious to enlighten a backward child, 'out of the many chicks Colt has pulled, you're the only one who's managed to tempt him to the altar. I'd given up all hope of seeing the boss take a tumble, but now that he has, I'd be willing to wager a year's salary that he'll never spare a glance for any other woman!'

Fortunately, when she walked on without speaking, he seemed to mistake her embarrassed blush for the shy awkwardness of a bride too new to marriage to find such intimate remarks acceptable, so tactfully he changed the subject.

'What's on our agenda today?' His enquiry was deliberately matter-of-fact. 'You've pointed out the best bird hides, shown me how to distinguish a stoat from a weasel—what about Brock the badger, how do I go about finding him?'

'It's highly unlikely that you'll ever see a badger in broad daylight,' she responded with relief. 'They wait until dusk before coming out to play, hunt for food, air old bedding and transport new grass, straw or bracken to their sleeping chambers.'

By the time she had located a patch of alders, favoured by badgers because they were partial to the berries, and pointed out copses and hedgerows most likely to house a sett, the drizzle had developed into a downpour, so in spite of wearing gear appropriate to the weather conditions they reluctantly decided to abandon their study of nature on the tacit understanding that it would be continued the following week.

Crouched low in the saddle, her head bent to avoid the slash of rain against her cheeks, she galloped Cello homeward, slackening pace only when they began cantering up the drive towards the stable yard. She was busily absorbed in the task of rubbing down the mare when she heard the squeal of brakes, the slam of a car door, then the crunch of booted feet approaching the stable. Expectantly she paused and raised her head just as Colt's towering frame appeared in the doorway.

'I've just seen Abe.' His voice sounded leashed, as if he were labouring under some kind of strain, then as his cold grey eyes raked her sodden figure he continued tightly, 'By the looks of him, he appears to have spent the entire afternoon wandering in the rain.'

'Oh . . .?' she quavered nervously, running her tongue around suddenly dry lips as she sensed seething anger, the threat of some sort of showdown. 'Is that so unusual?' she shrugged, trying to appear unconcerned. 'For that matter, so have I.'

'I must agree that walking in the rain can hardly be classed as unusual,' he replied, motionless as a wildcat poised to spring, 'neither is it strange that both you and he should choose to do so at the same time and in the same location. What does lead me to suspect that the arm of coincidence is being stretched too far is the fact that on the same day last week, and also during the previous week, Abe's car was parked on the very same spot at the exact times that you chose to exercise Cello. Have you been making secret liaisons, Rowan?'

His words dropped heavily as stones into a deep pool of silence.

'Don't be ridiculous!' she croaked, alarmed by his barely controlled fury.

With the hissing breath and snapping teeth of a predator he pounced, pinning her by the shoulders with her back against a wall.

'Then prove me wrong, Rowan!' He shook her vigorously in his temper. 'Tell me, what draws a dedicated Lothario to wander a lonely forest on every one of his days off?'

She stared appalled at the flint-eyed, fiery-haired demon whose iron control had never before been allowed to snap, tempted by sheer terror into betraying Abe's secret. But a reminder that Falstone honour was at stake gave her just enough courage to whisper:

'I . . . can't.'

The crush of his grip became so intense she almost cried out, then pain was superseded by unbearable remorse when his powerful frame shuddered and he stepped out of reach.

'Get out of my sight, Rowan!' he commanded in a harsh, rasping voice, 'while I'm still capable of resisting the temptation to wring your treacherous English neck!'

CHAPTER NINE

DURING the previous three days there had been heavy falls of snow, but as Rowan set out to keep her weekly date with Abe all that remained were a few white patches strewn over the higher fells while the hedgerows in the valley were lined with clumps of snowdrops, their delicate heads nodding bravely in a fresh spring breeze.

Deep in thought, she guided Cello through puddles of melted snow, over humped-back bridges crossing swollen streams, then skirted the edge of the forest where every now and then she passed stacks of long-handled beaters—fire-fighting equipment serving as a reminder that even summer brought its drawbacks—on her way towards a rise looking down upon a valley turned into a rubbish dump of piled-up ballast, hardcore, granite chippings, concrete blocks, and empty plastic bags enjoying a game of hide and seek with a playful wind. But for once, the din of working machinery, the shouts of men trying to make themselves heard, the glaring yellow cranes and matching steel bonnets of Colt's army of dam builders, caused her little concern as she brooded over his puzzling reaction to her last meeting with Abe.

After his explosive burst of anger had been doused, he had left her severely alone, returning to

the castle long after she had eaten a solitary dinner
and leaving each morning without breakfast,
before even Nanny was astir. Rowan gnawed her
bottom lip, wondering why she should be finding
his long absences so disturbing, puzzled by a sense
of rejection, bewildered by a strange feeling inside
her that she could not fathom, a tight knot of
yearning that kept her senses poised, leaping to
the sound of every footfall, every door slam, every
voice or movement that might be his.

But the worst time of all was night when she
lay wide awake straining to detect the slightest
sound of movement behind the door connecting
her bedroom with the comfortless dressing-room
containing a single narrow bed, which, ever since
their wedding night, Colt had chosen to occupy
in preference to a four-poster huge enough to
accommodate his large frame in comfort, spread
with lavender-scented sheets, lace-trimmed pil-
lowcases, downy blankets—and a painfully naïve
wife!

Mistaking the convulsive jerk of her wrists for
a tug upon the reins, Cello tossed back her head
and wheeled in the direction of the forest, heading
instinctively towards the path leading to the
clearing where each week she was usually left to
graze. But surprisingly, there was no sign of Abe,
who usually arrived first and sat patiently waiting.
When after an hour spent checking the bird hides
and looking for signs of any untoward disturb-
ance, he had still not put in an appearance, Rowan
was forced to the conclusion that he would not be
coming and dejectedly decided that rather than

return to the castle echoing with the noise of busy workmen she would make her way down to the village to ensure that all was well with a few of their elderly, less isolated tenants.

The first thing that struck her as she cantered past the line of cottages, the small garage with its two meagre petrol pumps, the solitary pub tucked small as a house beneath the spreading branches of a chestnut tree, was the lack of warmth in the villagers' greetings, the brief nods and quickly-averted glances that seemed to indicate some underlying grievance. A few paces onward, a glance towards the village store disturbed her further. The tiny stone built shop with its incongruous corrugated roof, faded paintwork and wooden nameplate bearing the barely discernible description: Hardware, Drapery, Grocer, Newsagent, had had its display window removed and the aperture filled with boarding that had scrawled across its surface: Business as Usual.

With a swift premonition that the occurrence had a connection with something unpleasant, she tethered Cello to a nearby post and hurried towards the entrance. The interior of the shop was so dark she felt temporarily blinded and for a moment could not distinguish the faces belonging to a babble of angry voices, but as her sight became adjusted she managed to single out Meg Storey, the shopkeeper, standing behind the counter with arms akimbo, holding forth to an audience of six that was cramming the shop to capacity.

'What happened to your window, Meg, has

there been some sort of accident?'

The miniature crowd fell silent and shuffled sideways to allow Rowan's slight figure access to the counter.

Meg bridled. 'Not an accident, Lady Rowan, but deliberate vandalism, I'm certain.' The usually placid woman sounded incensed. 'I'm sorry to have to say so, but we consider it was a sad day for all of us when your husband brought his steel-bonneted dam builders to our valley!'

A hearty chorus of 'Ayes!' underlined the villagers' bitter agreement with this statement.

'Vandalism? Surely not . . .?' Rowan faltered. 'Tell me exactly what happened.'

'The same thing as happens every Saturday night when those crazy dam-dogs are let off the leash!' a male voice boomed from the rear of the crush. 'They come tearing down to the village, a hundred or more at a time, fighting to get into a pub built to accommodate a dozen. Then after closing time when they've drunk themselves silly they start roistering around the village in search of girls, and when they can't find any—and parents make certain they don't!—they mark their disappointment by wrecking everything in sight!'

'Not the window . . .!' Rowan questioned faintly, her eyes pleading to be contradicted.

'And the street lamp,' Meg affirmed. 'It's been smashed to smithereens, leaving folk to grope their way to their own front doors!'

'And lighted cigarettes dropped into the letter-box!'

'And garden gates lifted off their hinges!'

'And what about the time they polluted the stream by emptying a drum of oil left on the garage forecourt!'

'And the noise of blaring horns as they race each other back to camp!'

'Don't forget old Archie's dog—for fourteen years it wandered the village streets, slow on his feet and blind as a bat, without coming to a ha'porth of harm, only to finish his days beneath the wheels of some maniac's car!'

'Stop, please!' Rowan clasped her hands over her ears to shut out the rising sound of resentment felt by villagers who seemed to be including herself among Kielder's band of culprits. 'I'm terribly sorry,' she gasped, backing towards the door. 'I'm certain my husband has no idea . . . I promise you that once he's been told the disturbances will cease.'

Shaking with reaction, she untethered Cello and climbed into the saddle, unnerved by a personal antipathy directed by villagers who had always treated her with respect, whom she had always considered to be her friends.

Flags of anger flew high in her cheeks as she headed Cello away from the village and began racing her in the direction of the dam, determined to search out Colt and spill out her grievances while resentment was still hot, while concern for the welfare of the villagers remained a whip to flog her flagging courage.

But after a hard, fast ride across the moor had cooled her temper instinct began counselling caution, reminding her of the need for steady nerves and a clear head when pleading her cause to a less than amenable husband. Acting upon impulse, she veered in the opposite direction, deciding that a visit to the Grahams would supply the interval of calm necessary before what might—depending upon Colt's uncertain humour—turn out to be a heated confrontation.

Dale was just about to step into her father's car when Rowan approached the farmhouse.

'Hello, Dale,' she greeted her, 'I didn't expect to see you home at this time of day!'

'Nor would you, as a rule, 'the girl sounded peculiarly sullen, 'but owing to pressure of work we've had to stay late at the office these past few evenings, so the boss insisted I took the morning off. I tried to argue that it's he who needs time off, that he can't continue indefinitely working eighteen hours a day, trouble or not, but he wouldn't listen.'

'Trouble . . .?' Rowan echoed stupidly.

'Don't you know?' Dale sent her a curious look. 'The workforce was on strike until yesterday— surely you noticed the absence of sound, the lack of movement? The valley was like a deserted battlefield.'

'Yes, of course,' Rowan stammered, lying to save face, to prevent Dale from guessing that as well as being denied the privilege of her husband's confidences she had been too wrapped up in her own affairs to notice the cessation of activity in the valley. She was spared the embarrassment of trying to appear knowledgeable about the cause of the strike when Dale defended hotly.

'The boss was very sympathetic towards the men's views, he did everything in his power to ensure that working conditions were made as comfortable as possible during a spell of atrocious weather by providing protective clothing, agreeing to shorter shift working and extra pay to compensate for the unusually difficult conditions, but still a tiny minority, encouraged by what I'm certain are a couple of professional troublemakers, held out for more, pressing for further concessions with tongue in cheek, knowing full well that their demands were outrageous! And of course,' Dale's glance grew even more unfriendly, 'the situation was not improved by Abe's absence. Had he still been here he could at least have relieved the boss of minor responsibilities.'

Rowan felt stunned, as if kicked by a bucking mule. 'Where has Abe gone?' she croaked. 'On holiday . . . on a business trip . . .?'

'I have no idea, Lady Rowan,' Dale turned her head aside, but not before Rowan caught a glimpse of tears. 'One day he was here and the next he had gone. I was hoping,' she hesitated to take a deep breath, then rounded defiantly, 'that as you and he have become so friendly lately you might be able to tell me.'

Rowan blushed scarlet. As in all small communities, rumour raged hot as a forest fire, but even so it had simply not occurred to her that her innocent meetings with Abe could be giving rise to speculative gossip—gossip that must somehow have drifted to Colt's ears, making him justifiably angry!

A little of this anger, together with a large amount of hauteur inherited from ancestors who had always been counted as being beyond criticism, was reflected in her cool rebuke.

'I consider it my duty to be approachable and friendly towards all my husband's employees; it's gratifying to learn that my efforts have been noted with approval. However, my level of involvement doesn't require me to keep tabs on employees' comings and goings. Abe quite properly has gone about his business knowing that I would neither require nor expect to be told of his intentions.'

Without bothering to dismount, she tugged on the reins, wheeling Cello about with the intention of retracing her steps. Pride was rampant, pride of race, pride of position, and a newly-provoked feminine pride that was baulking at the thought of anyone knowing that all was not well between herself and her husband.

'It's much later than I'd thought,' she glanced at her watch. 'Would you please convey my apologies to your mother and tell her I'll call again soon? Oh, yes,' she called airily across her shoulder as Cello began cantering out of the farmyard, 'and would you please tell my husband when you see him that I insist he returns home in time to have dinner with me this evening!'

As she and Cello sped towards the castle she found it hard to decide whether her heartbeats had become erratic because of anger or because of the prospect of Colt's reaction to her reckless demand for his presence. He was almost certain to read her message as a challenge—and be quick to accept!

The workmen had finished their jobs in the hall and all planks, trestles and scaffolding had been removed so that cleaners, under Nanny's supervision, could remove all traces of dust from walls and floor in preparation for the arrival of a second wave of invaders who were awaiting Colt's command to begin upon the task of restoration. As she crossed the hall, making towards the stairs, Nanny appeared bristling from the direction of the kitchen quarters, obviously having been on the alert for sounds of her arrival.

'What do you intend doing about those?' She pointed to a pile of cardboard boxes which, ever since their arrival some days earlier, had remained stacked in a corner. 'I'm tired of moving them around. What's inside, for heaven's sake?'

'Clothes,' Rowan replied succinctly, 'most probably a useless assortment of outfits that my misguided husband arranged to have sent from London fashion houses. I believe he was motivated by an urge to uncover hidden facets, Nanny,' she scoffed, 'the jewel in his crown is not shining half so brightly as he'd hoped!'

'A man can't be blamed for preferring a silk purse to a sow's ear!' Nanny scathed. 'But you no doubt intend continuing with your strategy of revenge by refusing to co-operate?'

'Certainly . . .' Rowan began, then suddenly changed her mind, '. . . not! Give me a hand to take them upstairs, out of your way.'

When all of the boxes—pale grey, featherlight, and tastefully decorated—had been deposited in her bedroom she stared at them thoughtfully. She had deliberately left them standing unopened in the hall where Colt was bound to see them in order to supply an extra bone of contention, a symbol of defiance with which she had hoped to shatter the silent armistice, so allowing the battle in which words replaced the stab of dirks to recommence. But although he could not have helped noticing the pile of boxes slowly gathering dust, he had remained uncharacteristically unresponsive. Was it, she wondered, because his anger was still seething? Or had the chauvinistic, egotistical war lord become weary of combat and conceded defeat? She frowned as an alternative thought crossed her mind. Had Abe and Dale been right in their assumption that Colt was being too far-stretched, that he was struggling with a load too heavy for any man—even the immortal Kielder?

Casting a freshly speculative eye over the pile of boxes, she was smote by conscience and made an impulsive decision. The question of Abe's sudden disappearance and the villagers' problems would have to wait. Colt's appeal for an amnesty had obviously been born of weariness—the claws of the lion had been cut, it seemed pointless to insist upon drawing his teeth!

Some time later when Nanny stepped inside a room knee-deep in tissue paper and empty boxes she gave a gasp of startled admiration. A vision of loveliness swung round to face her.

'Well, Nanny, what do you think?'

She looked long and hard at the girl whose

youthful beauty had remained cocooned by a preference for old, comfortable, and strictly functional clothes. But now the chrysalis had emerged, and with the aid of a diaphanous dress swirling, light, and shimmering with intricate detail, changing quickly as a mood from snow-white to pale pink as she moved beneath the light, had developed into an incredibly beautiful butterfly.

'Child . . .!' her voice trembled with proud emotion, 'you look as I've always wanted you to look—as I've always known you would look if ever you decided to take pains with your appearance.'

'You don't think the bodice is cut too low?' Immaturity showed as her fluttering, downcast lashes doubted the modesty of gently rounded breasts plunging into a tantalisingly deep cleavage.

'Not at all.' Nanny suppressed a smile of satisfaction at the thought of Kielder's reaction to a bride made to look ethereal and very desirable in a dream dress with a flattering neckline, full, wrist-length sleeves, and a deeply flounced skirt with a hand-span waistline wrapped twice by a wide sash belt. 'You'll do nicely.' She reverted to her usual irritable snap in case too much approval should scare the butterfly into discarding her finery. 'If the rest of the outfits are as comely you should find no cause for complaint.'

'They are—and I haven't!' Rowan's blue eyes sparkled with delight as they roved the selection of original, fashionable, brilliantly designed clothes made from materials ranging from pastel see-through chiffon to vibrant body-hugging jersey.

'They're all so stylish, and what's more, they couldn't fit more perfectly if I'd been measured for each one!'

'Good! Now help me to clean up this mess.' Nanny stooped and began gathering up tissue paper, ribbons and pins. 'If you like, as I've a while to spare before dinner, I'll do your hair just as I used to do your mother's whenever she and your father were to attend a dance or some important function.'

Exactly as she had expected, Rowan took fright.

'Oh, that's hardly necessary, Nanny! I might even decide to change—it's such a waste, don't you think, to wear a dress such as this just to spend an ordinary evening at home?'

Nanny straightened and for the first time that Rowan could recall pleaded quietly, 'Don't do me out of my treat, it's been such a long time since I've practised my skill as a lady's maid—please, child, humour me just this once?'

Whether the exercise was prolonged deliberately Rowan could not be certain, but by the time the old servant had finished brushing and pinning glossy coils of raven-black hair into a style that left a vulnerable nape bare and displayed to perfection a young, tender neckline and smooth slope of shoulders, the crunch of tyres on the gravelled driveway gave warning of Colt's approach. With suspiciously good timing, Nanny threw down the comb and rushed towards the door.

'You look perfect! I'll leave you now, I must

make sure that everything's as it should be in the kitchen!'

The advance of quick, firm footsteps along the passageway outside her room, the sound of movement from next door, then the gurglings and rumblings that erupted from ancient water pipes each time a bath was being drawn sent Rowan shivering towards a fire kept constantly replenished with logs in order to banish chill from the spacious bedroom. Now that confrontation was imminent she felt nervous, at a complete loss how to word the explanation Colt was bound to demand—so much so that when the door between their rooms was finally flung open and she swung round flustered to see him standing on the threshold, enquiring eyebrows winging, she could only manage to blurt.

'Thank you for the dresses . . .!'

'Thank you for finally deciding to accept my gift.' The drawl she had been dreading was missing, and as he advanced towards her she noted signs of strain around tight-set lips, in the fine network of lines that sprang into life as his eyes narrowed warily. Breath caught in her throat when a beam from an overhead lamp struck a glint of silver in his hair, reminding her of snow sprinkled lightly over autumn-red bracken. How right Abe and Dale had been to warn her! Colt looked taut enough to snap, so finely balanced a mere speck of sand might upset his equilibrium.

'Your hair is still damp.' As much to her own surprise as his she extended her hands to coax him closer to the fire. The moment their fingers

touched she realised her mistake, but when she
tried to pull away his grip fastened tight as the
jaws of a trap around her wrists. Immediately,
senses starved of contact began to writhe and
purr, the blush of firelight on her cheeks deepened
to a scorching inferno, then paled to the whiteness
of ash beneath the shocking coldness of a stare
that douched her from head to toe, missing not
one silken coil of hair, one quivering eyelash, one
trembling curve, one infinite quantity of milk-
pure skin left exposed by what she belatedly
realised was a far too revealing neckline.

'Once I was misguided enough to think you
meek, Rowan,' he grated rawly. 'I know now that
what I mistook for meekness is in reality an un-
common patience in planning a revenge that's
worthwhile. But let me warn you, before you
embark upon whichever devious exercise you have
in mind, that our clan's battle cry still remains:
"*Wha' dare meddle wi' me!*" '

As many had done before her, Rowan stiffened
with alarm at the menace contained in the war cry
of a clan chief who in days gone by had been
feared the length and breadth of the Border.

'I don't understand,' she gulped, feeling
shocked as a stray in the middle of a minefield. 'I
realise you've put the wrong interpretation on my
meetings with Abe and I'd explain fully if I could
do so without breaking my word. However, as
soon as I see Abe——'

'You won't be seeing Abe ever again.'

His cold shock of words left her gasping. 'I
won't—why not . . .?'

'He's been banished,' he astounded her by saying, looking flint-eyed and incredibly stern, 'found guilty of offending against Border law that decrees a man shall not cut down the trees of other men, sow his corn or feed his cattle on others' grass, nor,' roughly he pulled her into his arms until, pinned against his chest, she felt in danger of drowning in the depths of grey, storm lashed eyes, 'shall he cast covetous glances in the direction of other men's wives!'

'You're a barbarian,' she choked, wide-eyed with disbelief, 'in wickedness a league beyond the devil!'

He silenced her by planting an explosive kiss upon her wrecked mouth, lighting a fuse that blasted her defensive barricade to smithereens. Every deprived nerve responded by leaping to the touch of hands intent upon removing every silken obstacle between them and the slim, satin-skimmed body trembling with an urgency that began as fear then dissolved into ecstasy as his hungry lips traced a path of desire along a tender line of neck and shoulder, lingering against pulsating nerves, seeking, exploring, then finally coming to rest with a groan of anguish against a creamy, delicate curve of breast.

All will to fight became submerged by an urge to surrender, to lay down her arms and submit to becoming a prisoner of love—a word that never once, not even at the pinnacle of passion, had ever escaped his plundering lips. Tossed by a cataclysm of emotion, she clung to his powerful frame as he tortured her with kisses until her mouth felt crushed, her body racked, pride shattered by the indignity of being forced to plead humbly as a prisoner before a jailor.

'No, Colt, don't . . .! Punish me if you must, but in any other way but this!'

But his reiver blood was up, his veneer of polish stripped, laying bare material that was raw, tough, and ill to tame—a man bent upon practising the ancient Border code applying to property and theft: *'Reivers have a persuasion that all property is common by the law of nature and is therefore liable to be appropriated by them in their necessity'.*

Necessity was rife in slumbrous grey eyes when he lifted her into his arms and began carrying her towards the bed.

'Sweet simpleton!' he mocked without compassion her wide fearful eyes and tear-stained cheeks—pale as the lace-trimmed pillow beneath her head. 'Even the mildest-natured beast grows savage when fed only bread and water—surely, novice nun, you must have foreseen the outcome of issuing an invitation to dine, then setting a sumptuous meal before a man who's starving!'

CHAPTER TEN

ROWAN stopped dead in her tracks, halted by the sight of Colt enjoying a leisurely breakfast with a newspaper propped up against the coffee pot in front of his plate.

'Good morning, Rowan,' he greeted her with the ease of a friendly acquaintance, as if last night's torrid, earth-shattering encounter amid cool cotton sheets had never happened. 'I've decided to take the day off to go fishing—would you care to join me?'

She glanced out of the window at puffballs of cloud chasing across an expanse of brilliant blue sky; at a garden glowing golden with sunshine, spread from terrace to driveway, along borders and under trees with a carpet of nodding daffodils.

In spite of a heart heavy with pain, steps rendered leaden with the weight of an imaginary ball and chain, her lips refused to utter the refusal that pride demanded.

Something about her young, tragic figure drove him to his feet and sent him striding towards her. The sudden jolt of her reflexes when his finger tipped up her chin could have been mistaken for revulsion. Swiftly as sun disappearing behind cloud his smile faded, his eyes grew bleak, as he grated:

'Please . . .?'

She flinched out of reach of his lithe body, as far away as possible from muscles rippling beneath a shirt fitting sleek as a pelt, with sleeves rolled up over sinewed biceps and a collar falling open to expose a powerful neck and a wide expanse of wind-burnt chest. Denims slung low around narrow hips, cinched with a leather belt sporting a barbaric brass buckle, projected a prowling sexuality that refused to allow her respite from the memory of the sensuous moulding of her body against his, the sensation of power, the trembling weakness she had felt when satin-skinned muscles had knotted and writhed as if tormented by the tender stroke of her hands.

Huskily, keeping a spear's length between them, she conceded with the hot cheeks and trembling mouth of a coward: 'Thank you, I'd like to . . .'

Though that part of the river they had decided to fish was situated within the castle grounds, Colt told Nanny to prepare them a packed lunch and swore her to secrecy about their movements, insisting that all telephone enquiries and even personal callers, however urgent their needs, were to be instructed to call back tomorrow as today he could not possibly be reached.

Beware the Ides of March! A superstitious shiver ran down Rowan's spine as without apparent reason she recalled that the date was the fifteenth of March, the day Julius Caesar had been warned of impending and certain danger. But when Colt smiled and offered a hand to help her over a stile she shrugged off the premonition, determined to make the most of a day stolen from spring, a precious day of truce from the warring elements of winter.

Amid an atmosphere of untalkative neutrality they reached the river and began stalking the bank in search of a likely beat. Almost immediately, Colt spotted a patch of bubbles rising to the surface of the water, indication that a shoal of hungry bream were sucking and sifting for food along the muddy bottom.

With a grunt of satisfaction he slipped a haversack from his shoulder and unearthed a tinful of ground bait—stale bread soaked, squeezed dry and then mixed with meal—which he had hopefully prepared as a lure to encourage any shoal to linger.

Rowan left him searching for a tin of worms and made her way farther downstream to a stretch of easy water shadowed by trees and bushes. Carefully she crept through a tangle of undergrowth and baited a hook with cheese paste, a delicacy to which chub were extremely partial, letting it dibble on the surface, casting towards the sun so that her shadow would not fall upon the water.

Gradually her mood of slight depression gave way to contentment as sunshine began warming the earth and the scent of resin rose to mingle with woodsmoke drifting from some far-off bonfire. Excitement bounded when a chub began sucking in her bait, but she managed to curb her movements, waiting until the sturdy fish turned down before striking.

A couple of satisfying hours later Colt appeared carrying the luncheon basket and called out the usual fisherman's enquiry: 'Any luck?'

Proudly she responded with a nod, indicating a sizeable catch of chub, their scales glistening jade and silver in the sunlight.

'How have you done . . .?' For the first time that day she was able to meet his eyes without embarrassment.

'Just a couple of eels,' he told her ruefully, betraying a reluctance to admit himself beaten.

'I suspected you were being over-generous with ground bait,' she dared to tease. 'Bream are shy enough without encouraging them to be too lazy to rise!' She bubbled over with laughter when his expression grew wry, experiencing a heady sense of triumph at the knowledge that for once she had managed to outdo King Kielder.

'Bighead!' he accused so disgustedly that she burst out laughing, then when after a second's pause he joined in she felt a swift stab of pleasure, a certainty that this bright golden day was destined to be one of the happiest of her life.

With healthy appetites they attacked the meat and potato pasties, crusty rolls wrapped around thick slices of ham, crisp apples and chunks of crumbly cheese that Nanny had deemed a fitting accompaniment to a healthy outdoor pursuit. Then as they sipped white wine that Colt had chilled to perfection by embedding the bottle up to its neck in the gravelled riverbed, she gradually felt able to relax her guard, to talk freely and warmly about small inconsequential things.

'I do hope today marks the beginning of a long settled spell,' she mused, lying back replete, using her hands as a pillow beneath her head. Unaware that her words could have been misinterpreted as a wish for a lull in their stormy relationship, she sighed with contentment and allowed her lazy lids to droop, so missing his sharpened glance, his sudden jerk to attention. 'It very often happens that during a warm spell at this time of year half a clutch or more of precious eggs are laid, then along comes the night frost to kill any hope of the eggs being hatched. Even heavy rain is a hazard to early lambs who have no lanoline on their coats and need at least a week in dry conditions for their fleece to become waterproofed.'

As if anxious to reassure her, a feathered Romeo perched on the branch of a nearby tree began serenading his Juliet, a sweet penetrating trill that filled the air with a message of springtime, an anthem made poignant by a vital resurgence of the urge to mate. Her heart began racing as she listened, conscious of Colt's fixed stare, sensing that if only she dared to look she would discover his grey eyes transmitting the same thrilling, vibrant message sent by every male lusting after his mate.

When the tension threatened to become unbearable and a deep pink blush was beginning to betray her awareness of his magnetism, she made a cowardly effort to break the spell by jerking upright to enquire brightly:

'I do hope you saved your eels for Nanny, she

reckons they make a very tasty pie.'

Her tactic was deliberately devious, prompted by a suspicion that without his being aware of it, he had probably been inculcated during childhood with the deep-rooted prejudice against the eating of eels that was characteristic of all Scots. She had to force back a smile when his shudder of repugnance told her that her shot in the dark had landed on target.

'Which only strengthens my suspicion that you English are very far from particular in your feeding,' he responded with evident disgust.

'Nonsense!' Her lurking smile sprang into full existence. 'I think it's a shame that Scots allow prejudice to prevent them from taking advantage of the most plentiful and nutritious fish in our waters. I'm even willing to bet,' she nodded sagely, 'that most of you at some time or another have eaten an excellent "filleted sole" without being aware that you were actually eating eel.'

'I dispute that.' Much to her relief, his response was crisp, the heat of his tone well below danger level. 'The serpent is the symbol of the devil, and all Scots feel that the eel, being like a serpent, is a creature of evil influence and so must always remain taboo.'

'In case they should be accused of cannibalism?' The impudent retort left her lips without thought, and to her dismay seemed to change in flight from a light tease to a heavily poisoned barb. When his expression darkened she regretted the impulse that had revived all the resentment he had shown last evening after her hissed accusation: '*In wick-edness, you're a league beyond the devil!*'

'Whether it's true or false, what is said about a man often influences his actions,' he warned her grimly, rising to his feet. 'We'd better take a walk in case I should feel tempted to exercise the devil's prerogative to seek slaves and claim obedience. I think you will agree that our route should avoid highly evocative place names such as Murder's Rack, Hell Cauldron, Kielder's Edge and Thrust Pick!'

Feeling utterly miserable and close to tears, she followed in his wake along a path leading away from the river bank, so overgrown she often found it necessary to edge sideways through bramble thickets that scratched her face and ran thorny fingers through her hair, to pant up steep inclines then to be precipitated down muddy slopes before she had time to draw breath. A dozen times she was on the verge of giving up, deciding she was foolish trying to keep up with his deliberately punishing pace, but she doggedly persisted, following his progress through woodland with un-expected streams, uneven contours and endless variety of mosses, ferns, plants and trees that con-trasted like a shambles against the orderly, strictly regimented fir tree forest.

She had no way of knowing whether it was by accident or design that he discovered the well, but when she finally caught up and saw him peering down a circular, stone-rimmed aperture she felt a surge of hysteria as strong as she had felt on the day many years before when as a terrified child she had believed the well was destined to become her grave.

'Colt, be careful, please come away . . .!' Her strangled shout jerked him back from the rim to stare in long-drawn-out silence at a face white with shock, eyes dark with newly-resurrected horror.

'So you do remember,' he challenged softly, 'and all this time I've been thinking you'd forgotten.'

'I could never forget!' She expelled a long, shuddering breath. 'Nightmares keep fresh in my mind the horror of being enclosed within dark walls running with damp, slippery with slime, of lying covered in reeking mud, knowing that any minute I might slip and plunge for ever down a bottomless pit. It was only recently that Nanny told me that you were my rescuer, the one who saved me from the water kelpies!'

She knew she was babbling hysterically, giving way to cowardice, when a feverish ague attacked every limb and she had to clutch at a tree trunk to support knees buckling beneath her.

'Stop it, Rowan!' He reacted just in time to save her from falling. As he snatched her close, encircling her trembling body within the comforting circle of his arms, she fell quiet, reassured by the feel of powerful shoulders beneath her fretful hands.

'Fool that I am,' he condemned himself roughly, 'I should never have brought you here, yet I felt so certain that the well would have been filled in years ago—as it ought to have been, as it will be,' he decided, 'no later than tomorrow!'

She weakened to the stroke of his chin against her cheek, to a rough-velvet voice urging tenderly: 'But before that happens, I want you to try to overcome your fear that has its roots not so much in a nasty experience as in the vague warnings issued to us when we were children by elders who ought to have known better.

"*Always spit three times into the spring before drawing water, otherwise you will be dragged into the well by the water kelpies!*"

'Remember how terrified we all were at the very mention of the kelpies,' he mused lightly, trying to ease her tension. 'They were credited with powers of speech, but if the gift of a coin were to be thrown into the well the kelpies were miraculously propitiated to the point of granting a wish. Your subconscious must have retained your childish fear of those tales,' he told her gently, 'but I promise that the fear can be exorcised by walking up to the well and examining it thoroughly.'

'I won't go near the well! I can't . . .!'

'You must,' he insisted, 'if only to prove to yourself how little need you have to be scared— it's merely a hole in the ground, Rowan, and a fairly shallow one at that. Also,' he stressed grimly, 'there's no brother Nigel lurking in the background waiting to use you as a sacrifice to his monumental conceit.'

Reluctant to show cowardice in the face of such logic, Rowan allowed him to lead her towards the well and held on tightly to his hand while she nerved herself to peer over the edge into the bottomless pit of iniquity that had plagued her dreams since childhood.

'I can see the bottom!' she gasped. Feeling a strengthening sense of shame at her own timidity, she whirled round to confess, shamefaced: 'I've always believed the well to be bottomless, that I'd fallen on to a ledge . . .!'

Solemnly, his eyes alight with laughter, Colt sighed. 'There goes my cherished image of bravery! You *were* only five years old at the time, yet you displayed all the enchantment of Eve when you rewarded my rescue act with a ravishing kiss and a promise to love me for ever.'

'I did . . .' she faltered, blushing with the shyness of the child he remembered.

'Yes, Rowan,' he assured her in tone to match an expression grown suddenly grave, 'you certainly did.'

She had to disperse the ambience of intimacy that was playing riot with her emotions, to prove to him and to herself that she would never voluntarily give in to desire writhing like a snake between them, that the only way she could be taken was by force.

'You mustn't allow the memory of a childish outburst to embarrass you,' she told him, striving to sound lightly amused. 'I vaguely remember that even as a boy you showed signs of the ruthless, overbearing man you were later to become, a man whose dedication to the accumulation of power left him no time for the frivolous occupation of loving and being loved!'

He recoiled as if from a blow, the weariness

and strain of the past few days reappearing in a face that for most of the day had looked carefree and relaxed.

'That is unjustified criticism,' he countered, tight-lipped, 'simply another example of English unfairness.'

Impetuously, and completely without reason, she reacted in the manner of a child who, because she has seen a cherished object marred, decides to wreck it entirely. Bitter words spilled from her lips as every past grievance pushed and shoved to the forefront of her mind, anxious to claim its turn. 'By your own admission you returned to this place nursing resentment like a festering sore in order to exact revenge against a family you had been taught from infancy to hate. Were you not ruthless in your determination to blackmail me into marriage and overbearingly patronising to my brother once you became master of his estate? You bought yourself a bride, not to love and to cherish, but simply to display a superior Falstone as one of your worldly goods. Even your mistress, Diane,' she stormed, his lack of return fire giving her confidence, 'has admitted to Abe that you're incapable of fidelity, that once a woman has been taken she's discarded, reduced to being filed as a telephone number in your book of conquests!'

This jibe penetrated his tough hide. Ferocious hands grasped her shoulders as he gazed down, temper rearing, at her suddenly aghast face.

'How dare you discuss me with Abe!' He shook

her fiercely. 'In spite of the alliance you and he have formed, the secrets you share, I'd imagined that you possessed sufficient loyalty to avoid discussing your husband with an employee!'

'Why should a tyrant expect loyalty from a slave?' she spat, incapable of restraining bolting resentment that was rushing her headlong towards disaster. The peace of the woodland had flown, the clearing had turned into an arena containing clashing antagonists employing the cut and thrust of words in place of dirk and sword. 'King Kielder may reign, but for how long?' she jibed. 'His subjects are on the verge of rebellion against indignities inflicted by his army of rowdies; his second-in-command has been banished because of groundless suspicion; and though the King has managed to buy possession of lands and castle, he's unable to purchase the allegiance that's the prerogative of the rightful heir, my brother Nigel, Earl of Falstone!'

'An incorrigible snob,' he thrust back, 'a penniless parasite who's spent the last few years of his life draped across bars imbibing dry Martinis, clinging to the fringes of White's Club, Lloyds, the Polo Club, losing what little cash he had to spare over the green baize tables of gambling dens—a man ever-conscious of his social position, yet ever ready to shrug off the consequent responsibilities! I couldn't agree more with your supposition that a boy is a reflection of the man he's to become, for your brother has developed exactly along the lines of the character I observed years ago—a braggart, an egotistical bully who felt no qualms about putting his sister's life at risk for the sake of proving a point, but who became hoist by his own petard when he was shown up as a coward, too concerned for the safety of his own skin to even attempt a rescue. Do you really believe your brother capable of exciting admiration or respect?' he blasted, looking ready to choke the truth past her mutinous lips. 'My mother used to call you a "croodlin' doo",' his voice softened, 'a motherless dove left abandoned in a nest of vultures. Surely, Rowan, you must by now have recognised your brother as a rotten staff that none may lean on without risking a fall?'

She jerked out of his slackened grip, family pride outraged. Though Nigel had proved beyond doubt that he was deserving of condemnation, some inner devil lit a sparkle of indignation in her wide blue eyes, poured angry scorn into her indictment.

'If that's so, then why were you so eager to step into his shoes, to emulate his role even to the point of forcing a promise from him that he would coax his friends into accepting your hospitality immediately the castle has been renovated into a condition suited to your elevated status?'

'That plan was evolved solely for your benefit.' Smartly, Colt rejected the mantle of social climber. 'For too many years you've been left abandoned to isolation, cut off from parties, social chit-chat, from gaining experience in the art of conversation, denied the opportunity of learning how to dress, how to apply make-up, how to behave in a manner fitting to your position. My aim was to redress that wrong!'

Humiliated beyond belief by this sudden insight into his mind, this glimpse of the socially inadequate, rawly-naïve, shabbily dressed picture she presented before his eyes, Rowan lashed out in her pain:

'Undoubtedly there's truth in the rumour that every Kielder's right hand belongs to the devil! When you were christened,' she condemned low and emphatically, 'some over-zealous relative must have contrived to exclude your heart as well as your hand from the baptism!'

She gained no sense of comfort from his recoil, or from lines of weariness etched deep as newly-inflicted scars upon his expressionless face. Defeat was an anathema to the proud Kielder, yet though his lance-straight body remained still, not a muscle twitched, she sensed defeat in his cold, unemotional decree.

'I had expected much of today, Rowan—obviously too much. But if business life has taught me anything, it's that there's a time to press on and a time to cut one's losses. For the fi_st time in my life I'm being forced to face failure, to concede victory to superior forces.' A hush fell over the clearing, birds fell silent, not a leaf stirred, no movement disturbed the winter-crisped bracken that housed countless small creatures, so that his apology fell flat and unfeeling into the breath-held air.

'I'm sorry I parted you and Abe. Because I'm responsible for the completion of the dam I can't do the gentlemanly thing and remove myself from your vicinity. What I can do is send a message to Abe telling him to return immediately. If he responds quickly—as I've no doubt he will—you two should be reunited some time tomorrow.'

CHAPTER ELEVEN

'KIELDER's gone!' Nanny's voice was harshly condemnatory. 'He's packed most of his things and left instructions that any mail should be forwarded to his office on the site. What's gone wrong, what foolishness have you been up to, bairn?'

As a result of a sleepness night caused by thoughts in a turmoil, by emotions twisting and writhing like a bucketful of eels, Rowan's face looked pinched with misery, her heart heavy with a sense of loss even greater than the anguish she had been caused by her brother's treachery. In the manner of a suffering animal seeking solitude in which to lick its wounds, she tried to escape Nanny's probing by making towards the door, but Nanny had no intention of being foiled from having her say.

Twitching the cover over the huge bed on which only one pillow was ever indented, only a minute area of bedsheet was ever crumpled, she sighed.

'The opportunity God sends is wasted on a sleeper! When will you waken up to the realities of life, child, and be grateful for your blessings?'

The indictment stung. Rowan did not feel blessed, more like cursed. 'As I'm so blind to my blessings, Nanny, perhaps you'd be good enough to enumerate them?'

Nanny faced her with arms akimbo, ready to bristle, but changed her mind when a glance at Rowan's face betrayed confusion and deep unhappiness.

'You've managed to keep the home you couldn't bear to part with,' she pointed out gently, 'you have the comfort of knowing that elderly tenants will never be evicted from their homes; you have health, wealth, and,' she hesitated for barely a second, 'a husband who loves you.'

Rowan's laughter rang hollow as she swung away from Nanny's far-seeing eyes and walked across to the window to stare at a view of fells and woodland shimmering through a haze of tears.

'You used to be perceptive as a witch,' she choked, 'and a loyal friend to my family, but your strange allegiance to Kielder has distorted your vision, Nanny, for I fear that you now see only what you want to see. You can't pretend to have forgotten that he bought me, the castle and its estate, purely as an act of revenge.'

'I must admit that at first I was fooled, just as you were, into thinking so, but not for long.'

The old woman's tone of complacency sent Rowan swinging round, bewildered. 'What are you suggesting?'

'I'm not merely suggesting,' Nanny snapped with a return to her usual no-nonsense manner, 'I'm offering a conclusion from the evidence of my own eyes! I've seen the way Kielder looks at you when he thinks he's unobserved, the way . . . the way a pauper might look at a banquet, or with the wistful, yearning look of a boy staring through a toy shop window knowing he can look but never touch. Ask yourself,' she almost snorted, 'what use has a man like Kielder, who's become accustomed to living well, for a rambling, draughty castle lacking every modern convenience? Though you were the last to hear of it, your brother made no secret of his intention to sell. Kielder bought this castle to prevent it from falling into strange hands, because he wanted to make you happy— and I'm willing to wager that he married you for exactly the same reason!'

After Nanny had slipped quietly out of the room Rowan slumped down upon the bed, her stunned mind hovering between derisive rejection and a surprising eagerness to believe the astonishing conclusion. She strove to be sensible, to marshal her arguments as a general would marshal his troops.

Colt had never once been unkind—but he had often shown impatience, even occasional fury.

Nanny was correct in her assumption that he was in some ways a sybarite, one who accepted luxury almost as a divine right—yet fable had it that sybarites had expected everyone to dance to their tune, so much so that even their horses had been trained to dance to the pipe.

Colt was a roistering reiver, a swinge-buckler, always ready and eager for a fight—yet though his sword and buckler had swashed and swinged with a great show of strength, she had emerged from each battle unhurt. All but twice . . .

She flinched from recalling the two nights she had spent in his arms, but forced herself to remember every detail, every passionate moment, feeding hope on the assurance that no man could have acted with such tenderness, concern, and sensuous ardour towards a woman he did not love. On the verge of being convinced, she cupped scorching cheeks between trembling hands, trying to impose a band of caution around her pounding heart and riotous senses, and succeeding only too well when the voice of prudence whispered: 'Love is hate's emotional twin—those whom we can love we find easy to hate.'

Both passionate interludes had been initiated by Colt's fierce anger!

Seeking her usual antidote to depression, she saddled Cello and set off in the direction of the forest. Feeling the absence of motivation, her limp-wristed pressure on the reins, Cello chose the path leading straight into the clearing where they had become accustomed to meeting Abe. Rowan's involuntary jerk when she saw him strolling aimlessly, obviously awaiting her appearance, seemed to surprise him.

'I'm sorry if I startled you,' he frowned. 'Weren't you expecting me? I've just left Colt; he implied that you would meet me here.'

He looked uneasy, his usual grin replaced by a thin-lipped line of worry.

'What did Colt say exactly?' Slowly Rowan dismounted and patted Cello's rump, encouraging her to graze.

'Nothing that made much sense—I only wish he had! Tell me, Lady Rowan,' he appealed desperately, 'what's gone wrong between Colt and me? I've no notion why, but his attitude towards me has undergone a complete change. There was even a time,' he gulped nervously, 'when he looked ready to beat the hell out of me—sometimes I wish he had, instead of banishing me without a word of explanation into the wilderness of Wales, supposedly to add scope to my work experience but basically, I suspect, because he can no longer stand the sight of me! Yesterday, when I received a message to return here immediately I thought my transgressions, whatever they might be, had been forgiven. Naturally I responded as quickly as I was able, driving all through the night, not even sparing the time to have a shave,' ruefully he ran his fingers through a stubble of beard, 'yet when I finally did meet up with the boss I found that nothing had changed. In fact, although I'd imagined it impossible his attitude was several degrees frostier!'

'Colt has been working under a great deal of strain,' Rowan faltered lamely, realising that he had not the slightest inkling of the real reason behind Colt's actions. Reluctant to upset him further by explaining in detail, she decided to tread warily, to elicit as much information as possible without revealing the true circumstances.

'Didn't he tell you about the strike? I know he could have done with your help; he's probably asked you to return in case there should be further trouble on the site. I believe that long after such incidents, resentments remain simmering and are apt to flare up anew at the slightest provocation.'

'Thanks for the vote of confidence,' he smiled

wryly, 'but I think you know as well as I do, Lady
Rowan, that Colt needs no help to win his battles,
he thrives on conflict and invariably emerges vic-
torious.'

Gingerly as a kitten she side-stepped the subject
and veered on a different course. 'As you stated
some time ago, Colt is working far too hard and
as a result he's over-reacting to upsets which
normally he would shrug off. Can you pinpoint
the actual occasion when his attitude changed?'

'I sure can,' Abe nodded emphatically, 'it was
the day you and I last met here in the forest. After
leaving you, I made my way back to the car and
found him parked alongside, almost as if he'd
been waiting for me. Immediately I appeared he
strode to meet me looking thunderous, and asked
what reason I had for coming to the forest on my
every day off. As he seemed in no mood to believe
me capable of taking up any outdoor hobby, I
evaded the question, and as you'd sworn me to
secrecy about the orchids I could give him no
convincing reason why you made weekly visits to
the same spot. He then drove off looking murder-
ous. That same night I received my marching
orders.'

His brow wrinkled as, deeply perplexed, he
tried to fathom Colt's unreasonable show of animosity. Then suddenly he jerked erect, squaring
his shoulders as if arriving at some decision.

'I'm going to have it out with him!' he
exploded, so violently Rowan jumped. 'I'll demand an explanation and refuse to budge until the
cross-grained, horny buzzard has given me one!'

He began striding purposefully out of the clearing, then paused to cast an apologetic smile across his shoulder. 'Heck, Lady Rowan, I'm sorry if I came over a bit strong—I know how much you love the guy . . .'

It was a long time before Rowan was able to move. Shock held her stunned, afraid as a cripple who has been miraculously healed yet is afraid to trust his limbs in case the happiness that beckoned should prove to be unreal, a figment of the imagination. Just a few words, one casually-worded sentence, had cured her of an inherited affliction, an inability to look kindly upon any Scot, and especially a Kielder; a determination to settle old scores, to nurse old grievances, to sacrifice herself as a martyr to the cause of family honour, when all the time, deep in her subconscious, had lain buried feelings too traitorous ever to be exhumed. Abe's careless pick of words had penetrated the deep crust of prejudice and heaved them to the surface, so that she could no longer deny herself the glorious relief of admitting to herself that she *really did love the guy*!

The transition from inertia to animation was swift once the realisation struck her that Abe, ignorant of his role of devil's advocate, was rushing to destroy her last tenuous chance of happiness. Colt's pride had been battered, was as weathered as the Kielder Stone. To be forced to apologise and to publicly admit to a marriage gone badly wrong would be bound to topple him into a state of lasting bitterness!

She rode swift as a Valkyrie towards the mêlée

of battle, racing Cello out of the forest, across wide stretches of marshland and over the shoulders of fells, chancing every treacherous short-cut in an effort to overcome the time lapse and arrive at the dam before Abe.

A sob of relief blocked her throat when she breasted a rise and saw his car moving slowly along the gravelled road leading down to the base of the plateau.

'C'mon, Cello!' she urged through gritted teeth as she encouraged the mare down a slippery slope strewn with boulders. 'I wouldn't normally ask you to risk damaging a forelock, but it's vitally important that we get to Colt first!'

As if horse-sense had managed to communicate that her mistress's future happiness was at stake, Cello responded with surefooted speed, negotiating all obstacles, then racing flat out across the floor of the valley. The contest between flying hooves and speeding wheels ended in a dead heat on the fringe of a crowd of muttering workmen and strangely-idle machinery. She sensed that something was wrong even before Abe's snapped enquiry:

'What's going on? Why aren't you sodbursters working?'

The nearest group of workmen spun round to face him, their mud-spattered faces solemn, anxious eyes shaded by the steel rims of protective helmets.

'There's been a cave-in in one of the tunnels!'

Rowan's heart leapt, anticipating the workman's final horrifying words. 'Kielder's in there, but whether he's been buried by the fall or trapped in the tunnel behind it, we don't know yet.' One of his companions nudged his elbow and nodded, indicating Rowan's tragically immobile presence. 'I'm sorry, ma'am,' the speaker mumbled, 'I wouldn't have broken the news so bluntly ... I didn't know you were there ... Don't you worry,' he attempted to sound hearty, 'we'll get the boss out, never fear.'

But fear was already clawing at her heart. 'You *must*!' she gasped, gouging desperate fingers into Abe's arm. 'Why is everyone standing about, why aren't they *doing* something?'

White to the lips, Abe put his arm around her shoulders and began guiding her through the crowd of hushed, subdued workmen, dispensing with any time-wasting attempt to get her to return home and wait for news.

'The tunnel in question is over a mile long but less than ten feet in diameter,' he explained, hurrying her through a parting of workmen. 'Colt's been worried about its safety for some time, slight rock showers and a constant fall of dust have indicated an unreliable stratum, which is why he was anxious for the concreting to begin, why he carried out periodic inspections to ensure that safety precautions were being observed to the letter. In all probability that's what he would be doing when the cave-in occurred.'

He bit off his words when the fringe of the crowd parted and they were abruptly confronted by a mass of granite boulders spilling out of the tunnel. Half a dozen men were sweating shoulder to shoulder, their helmeted heads ducking beneath naked light bulbs strung on wires fastened to the roof of the tunnel, clawing, heaving, grunting in the confined space, progressing slowly and cautiously in case one uncharted move, the dislodging of a buttress, should precipitate a second fall of rock.

'Oh, Colt . . .!' Rowan's despairing sob caused Abe to wince. 'You *can't* be, you *mustn't* be buried beneath all that rock!'

Keeping an arm wrapped tightly around her shaking shoulders, Abe called out to a man directing the rescue operation:

'How's it going?'

Muttering a hasty instruction to his second in command, the man clambered down the rock pile towards them. His features were unrecognisable beneath a layer of grime and sweat, but Rowan's pleading eyes found a small trace of comfort in an expression set with determination, in a tone of voice echoing with a cautious optimism she sensed was not adopted for her ears alone.

'As you'll probably appreciate,' he addressed Abe, but kept pitying eyes upon Rowan's agonised face, 'we're having to proceed slowly and with extreme caution, but we've managed to clear a gap at the narrowest part of the rockfall where it meets the roof of the tunnel, so creating an airflow which alleviates our most pressing problem, that of ensuring that the boss is in no danger of suffocating however long it might take us to free him.'

If he's still alive!

The unspoken doubt hovered in the air between them and was written upon the grave faces of men used to facing danger every day of their working lives, men as tough as the granite they blasted from the quarries, as basic as bedrock uncovered by the steel teeth and blades of their mechanical monsters. Yet many of them were having to swallow hard to disperse lumps in their throats; some were using the backs of grimy hands to brush away tears which, if challenged, they would have sworn were beads of sweat.

As if from a far distance, Rowan heard her own surprisingly steady voice querying: 'Is there any chance that you might be mistaken about Colt being trapped inside the tunnel?'

The man to whom she had appealed grimaced painfully, then cleared his throat. 'I'm afraid not, ma'am—he and I were just about to go inside the tunnel together when I turned back to issue instructions to a ganger, he was mere seconds in front of me when part of the roof caved in, but whether he was caught beneath the fall or merely trapped behind the blockage is what we have yet to discover.'

'I have an idea!' Abe peered into the mouth of the tunnel, his gaze fixed upon the site of operation. 'I reckon that gap you've opened up might just be wide enough to allow a man through. There's just a chance,' he glanced apologetically at Rowan, 'that Colt might be lying injured, in need of first aid. Every second might count!'

'We've already considered that course of action and discarded it as being too risky.' Rowan's surge of hope was depressed by the grated rejection. 'The weight of a man's body could exert sufficient pressure to dislodge a vital cornerstone in this jigsaw of rocks and send tons of stone tumbling inward. The weight of one boulder dropped from a height could crush a man's skull as easily as a hammer could flatten a matchbox.'

'Dear Rowan, so slim and slight you barely cast a shadow—I swear your supple, silk-clad limbs could be threaded through the eye of a needle!' Rowan cringed from the painful recollection of Colt's teasing words.

Instinct cautioned her to hold a tight rein upon an hysterical desire to scream at men who seemed content to stand gossiping while her husband could be dying, his life-blood slowly seeping away. Somehow she had to rejuvenate these plodding, slow-moving men, had to make them see her not as a woman, but as an instrument that might have been fashioned especially for such a situation.

'I could do it!' Even she was amazed by the strength of purpose running through her words.

'You?' Abe swung round, astounded. 'I couldn't possibly allow it, Colt would have my guts for——'

'I can ... I must!' she insisted, hanging on grimly to control.

'But, ma'am, it's far too dangerous—we don't know what conditions are like behind the barrier, and even if you did manage to wriggle your way through without mishap, you might be injured, even killed, by a second fall of rock!'

Calmly, almost as if she were sympathising with the man for his lack of insight, she reminded the worried overseer: 'And if Colt is behind there so might he be!' Then, so simply and convincingly that they were rendered bereft of further argument, she confessed what was in her heart, what she had only just admitted to herself. 'In which case my life wouldn't matter, because without Colt existence would become meaningless, I'd have no reason left for living.'

There was not one man present whose expression was not full of admiration for the slight, courageous girl who could hardly bear to wait until a makeshift harness had been fashioned from rope and fitted over her shoulders and beneath her armpits so that once she had negotiated the gap she could be lowered without risk of injury on to the floor of the tunnel; not one man whose horny fists did not knot with fear for her safety when with her pockets stuffed with various items of first aid and with a powerful torch secured to a broad leather belt fastened around her waist, she was given help to clamber up the pile of loose rock before she dropped to her knees and began inching along on all fours through the dark aperture, out of reach of helpless watchers.

Abe's voice, sounding demented with worry, encouraged her passage through the tight tunnel of rock with jagged points that gouged into her shoulders and pierced sharp as daggers through leather pads strapped around her knees. He was holding the rope attached to her harness, feeding it inch by inch through his fingers as she moved.

'Don't hurry, Lady Rowan, take it as slowly as you can, feel out every bit of rock in front of you before you move! When you're through the barrier give a tug on the rope so I'll know when to begin lowering you down into the tunnel!'

She made no attempt to reply. If her whole mind and being had not been centred upon reaching Colt she might have been overwhelmed by the panic-stricken horror of once again being entombed as she had been on the occasion, many years before, when Colt had been her rescuer. Now, as then, the darkness was intense, the atmosphere of danger oppressive, the fear of being buried alive in a tunnel of stone lurked hysterical as a scream in the back of her mind. But this time it was she who had been cast in the role of rescuer, she who had to maintain control over an ice-cool mind and precise, carefully deliberated actions, because her love for Colt transcended all fear, because his life and her future happiness depended upon the outcome of the exercise.

A hiss of fright escaped her tight lips when the ground fell away beneath her groping hands. Gingerly she eased one hand behind her back to give a tug upon the lifeline, and immediately Abe responded:

'You're through!' His far-off voice sounded choked. 'Now for the tricky part. Wriggle your way forward until your legs are clear of the rocks—don't be afraid of falling, the harness will hold your weight and there are three hundred guys out here all itching to take the strain on the rope. Do you understand, Lady Rowan? For

Pete's sake, if you're in any difficulty give us a yell!'

She tried to respond, then discovered to her horror that she could not. Tension had a grip upon her vocal chords, dust was clogging her nostrils and though her teeth were gritted, her lips tightly compressed, the taste of dust was acrid on her tongue.

'I'm all right!' she finally managed to croak, then, impelled by a sense of urgency, she sucked in a current of clean air and yelled. 'Everything's fine, let's get on with it!'

Seconds later she was dangling over the edge, swinging in mid-air with the wall of rock behind her. Slowly, jerkily, she was lowered to the floor of the tunnel. Immediately her feet touched the ground she discarded the harness and groped for her torch. The beam of light wavered as erratically as her trembling hands around two solid walls bearing signs of construction; over the barrier of rock through which she had crawled, then into a maw of darkness where the remainder of the tunnel stretched. She tightened her grip upon the torch and pointed the beam downwards, mumbling a desperate prayer for Colt's safety as she scoured the floor for some sign of him.

When the beam of light fell upon a jacket sleeve, a sheepskin collar, then burst like flame around a fiery, belovedly-familiar head, a wave of relief weakened her courage and her vision was blinded by a swift, hot spill of tears. Fiercely she blinked them away and sank down on her knees beside the inert figure lying with arms outflung, eyes closed, and one leg buried to just below the knee beneath a fringe of fallen debris.

'Colt!' She bent over him sobbing, showering tears of grief and relief upon his senseless head. 'Oh, God, he mustn't die! Please let him live for my sake!'

Reminded of the purpose of her mission, she exerted a tight rein upon her emotions and steeled herself to carry out the instructions she had been given, looking for signs of bleeding, for evidence of serious injury, sliding a trembling hand against his neck and being rewarded with the discovery of a faint but steady pulsebeat.

'What's happened down there?' Abe's voice echoed around the pitch-black cavern, demanding an immediate answer.

'I've found him!' she responded in a high-pitched cry, tremulous with delight. 'He's alive and in no immediate danger, but please, Abe, tell the men to hurry, we must get him out of here!'

CHAPTER TWELVE

LIFE inside the castle had reverted almost to normal. All work of interior restoration had been suspended in order to ensure that peace and quiet, that was an essential aid to the master of Falstone's recovery from severe concussion, could be strictly maintained. Mercifully, his only other injuries were a broken leg and a bump on the forehead sustained when a glancing blow from a falling rock had knocked him unconscious. Now all he needed was time to heal his wounds and patience to withstand idleness forced upon him by the doctor's strict injunction to rest quietly with his mind relieved of business matters and his injured leg, encased in plaster, subjected to the minimum of pressure.

But during the week that had passed since his accident Colt had proved beyond doubt that patience was not one of his virtues, and as Rowan crossed the hall she winced from a hail of words being let loose behind the door of the master bedroom and hesitated, expecting the worst, when a door slammed, preceding someone's hasty exit from his room. Training anxious eyes upwards, she waited and saw Abe, looking red-faced and furious, rushing down the stairs towards her.

'What on earth's going on?' she began scolding. 'Surely you're aware that the doctor has insisted upon Colt having the maximum of peace and quiet?'

'In which case, it's a pity he wasn't left in the tunnel,' Abe snarled in aggravation.

'How can you say such a thing!' Her cry of reproach caused him a shrug of discomfort.

'Heck, I'm sorry, Lady Rowan, but the guy's turned dead mean, pouncing like a frustrated tiger upon anyone foolish enough to enter his lair! In spite of the doctor's instructions to the contrary, he insists upon receiving a daily report on the dam's progress, yet nothing I do or say seems to meet with his approval. In fact,' he clamped, looking suddenly accusing, 'just a few moments ago when I made some reference to your bravery—having no notion that he'd been kept completely in the dark about the part you played in his rescue—his temper reached flashpoint. I'm to consider myself fired,' he concluded bitterly, 'together with every other man on his staff who was, to quote his own words, *criminally irresponsible, slow-witted*, and *cowardly* enough to allow you to put your life in jeopardy!'

'Oh, Abe, I'm sorry!' she gasped. 'Perhaps I'm to blame for his ill-humour. He does hate being isolated—mindful of doctor's orders to ensure that he's forced to rest and to talk as little as possible, I've visited him myself only when I was sure he was asleep. But I promise I'll explain to him that you and the rest of the men were given no choice, that I was so determined to do what I did that nothing you could have said or done would have forced me to change my mind. Please,' she begged, 'don't mention a word about dismissal to the others until I've had a chance to speak to Colt.'

'Very well, if you say so, Lady Rowan.' His expression was a mixture of relief and puzzlement. 'But I'd advise you to get your timing right—to wait until after the brute's been fed, perhaps, when with luck you may find him purring!'

When Abe had taken his leave she wandered into the morning room, stalling for time, anxious to sort out her thoughts. She could not explain even to herself her reluctance to come face to face with Colt. She loved him desperately. During the hours she had sat on the floor of the tunnel with his head cradled upon her knee, numb with worry, stiff with cold seeping into her bones, that fact had been forcibly rammed home. Though the men had worked like beavers, it had taken long, painstaking hours to clear a way through the rock barrier, and during that time, while Colt had remained unconscious, she had had time to think, time to plumb the depths of the love she felt for the husband she had almost lost—could still be in danger of losing—and to realise that although he had given her no grounds for hoping her love might be returned, she would be content to exist for the rest of her life on any morsels tossed from King Kielder's table.

As she had kept watch by his bedside day and night for the first few anxious days after his accident, hope had been encouraged by the number of times her name had been mumbled past his lips, yet immediately he had begun showing signs of recovery she had shied from confronting his grey, enquiring eyes and had bolted from the room, returning to hover only when she was certain he was asleep, gazing hungrily, her heart in her eyes, before flitting away silent as a wraith whenever the flickering of eyelashes or a lightening of his breathing had warned that he was on the verge of awakening.

She was jerked from her reverie by the sound of a second commotion. This time his victim was Nanny. Bristling, panting with indignation, she flung open the door and stood quivering on the threshold clutching an armful of crumpled bed-linen.

'I can't stand another minute of this!' She glared at Rowan as if holding her personally responsible for Colt's ill humour. 'He's found fault with every meal I've set in front of him; he's refused to obey the doctor's orders and now,' she quivered visibly, 'he's insisting upon returning to his own bed, saying he absolutely refuses to spend another day propped up like a doll against lace-frilled pillows! For days he's been enquiring about your whereabouts, demanding to see you,' she accused. 'For heaven's sake, bairn, do as he asks, then we might all get some peace!'

'I will, Nanny,' Rowan decided quietly, realising that the moment of reckoning could be delayed no longer. 'Just give me a few more minutes and I promise I'll do as you ask.'

When a slightly mollified Nanny had withdrawn, closing the door behind her, Rowan drew in a deep, steadying breath and clenched her fists tight, willing fluttering nerves to subside, her wildly pounding heart to revert to its normal beat. Then she squared her shoulders and swung towards the door, but before she could step forward it crashed open, revealing Colt smouldering dangerously on the threshold.

'You shouldn't be out of bed,' she faltered, stunned by the shock of seeing his powerful frame supported by a stick; by a face contrasting deathly pale against the dark silk of his dressing gown, and by a livid bruise forking like lightning over stormy grey eyes.

'No, I should not,' he agreed savagely. 'In fact, I imagine my doctor, if he should see me now, would be appalled. But you left me no choice, did you, Rowan?' She backed away when he stomped inside the room, visibly aggravated by a restricting plaster cast. 'As you didn't bother to respond to any of my messages I was forced to come in search of you.'

'Please sit down, Colt,' she trembled, near to tears. 'I was just about to visit you, I would have done so sooner ... I never dreamt you'd be so foolish!'

'Didn't you, Rowan...?' When suddenly he dropped into a chair all fire seemed to die out of him. 'Isn't that how I've always appeared in your eyes—a jester aping a king; a rich clown who imagines money can buy him love?'

'No, Colt,' she whispered through a throat so tight it hurt. She was standing a few feet away from him with head downcast, nervous fingers lacing, bruise-dark lashes spiked with tears. 'Far from appearing foolish, you've always struck me as being an extremely rational person, one who's sure of his aims and certain how best to achieve them.'

She winced when harsh laughter grated from his lips, recoiled from a question thrown contemptuously as a bone to a grovelling hound. 'Do I look like a man who has everything he wants? I climbed high and fell low,' he admitted with a grimace of defeat that was completely alien to his character, 'some might say that I've received the just deserts of an upstart crow who pressed his suit upon an unwilling dove.' He rose to his feet looking spent, utterly weary. 'Abe told me about the part you played in my rescue,' he clipped so coldly she flinched. 'Your actions were foolhardy, nevertheless I'm grateful for the concern you must obviously have felt.'

Rowan's taut string of endurance suddenly snapped. 'So grateful that you've threatened to fire every man who struggled to save your life?' she flared. 'What makes you so blind, Colt, so insensitive to love?'

His stick clattered to the floor as he grabbed her close to hiss. 'They allowed you to put your life at risk—I'll never forgive them for that!'

The heavy thud of heartbeats filled the silent room while their glances clashed, held, probed, then became transfixed, startled by a glimpse of reality too ethereal to be believed. It took all the courage she possessed to chance being rebuffed, becoming an object of pity or, worse still, ridicule.

'The men tried hard to stop me, Colt,' she told him simply, 'until I explained that if you were to die I should have no wish to live.'

She had not thought it possible for his pallor to increase, for a quiver to rake across a mouth so hardbitten.

'Don't feel sorry for me, Rowan,' he threatened. 'I can take anything but pity!'

'Then take my love, Colt,' she pleaded, laying her defeated head against a dark silk lapel, 'for pity's sake, take my love!'

Her heart responded with a leap to the crush of arms savage with longing, to kisses that drowned her in ecstasy, to passion that swept her off her feet, lifted her, tossed and buffeted, into a stormy vortex of desire that drained her of misgivings and convinced her beyond doubt of his urgent, violent need.

'You *do* love me . . .!' she accused dreamily when he finally allowed her to draw breath.

'And have done for most of my life,' he breathed the shaken confession. 'Even when I was a child, you represented the unattainable, a being as rare and distant as a princess in an ivory tower. For many years,' he whispered against her still, attentive ear, 'I've travelled the world with your image stamped upon my heart—a memory so treasured no other woman could live up to it, a dream so fragile, so desirable, that I was almost afraid to return in case I should find you changed. You are the present I've saved up all my life for, my darling, and I found you exactly as I'd hoped, as unspoiled and untainted as the animals and birds you so fiercely protected. Unchanged in every respect,' he loosened tender, trapping arms to administer a gentle shake, 'to the point of having retained your mistrust of Scots, and of a Kielder in particular. You put up a hard fight,' he sighed, his eyes clouding with painful memory, 'a fight I felt certain I'd lost when you charged me with blackmail and accused me of spending money in an attempt to purchase love.'

'A love that you'd already won, King Kielder,' admonished his most faithful and loving subject, 'a love born on the night of the hunter's moon that will shine constant as sunrise every day of the rest of my life.'

Filled with remorse by this reminder of a night when desire had overruled the demands of conscience, humbled by her generous refusal to condemn, Colt hugged her slender body close and with his eyes fixed hungrily upon a mouth sweet as honey, groaned in an agony of loving contrition the words she had waited so long to hear. 'Precious croodlin' doo! If only I could tell you how much I love you—if only I could tell you *all*!'

A WORD ABOUT THE AUTHOR

Margaret Rome's first Harlequin was published in 1969. Appropriately, it was entitled *A Chance to Win* (Harlequin Romance #1307).

But her chance was a while in coming. In her teens Margaret dealt with a long-term bout of rheumatic fever; then followed a series of manual jobs that "just could not satisfy my active mind," and finally marriage and the birth of a son. But at last, when Margaret did get down to the business of writing—beginning by doodling with pen and paper—she discovered that a sentence formed, a second one followed, and before long, paragraphs had developed into a chapter. "I had begun the first of many journeys," she says.

Today Margaret and her husband make their home in Northern England. For recreation they enjoy an occasional night out dancing, and on weekends they drive into the beautiful Lake District and embark on long, invigorating walks.

NOW...

8 NEW

Harlequin Presents...

EVERY MONTH!

Romance readers everywhere have
expressed their delight with Harlequin
Presents, along with their wish for
more of these outstanding novels by
world-famous romance authors. Harlequin is
proud to meet this growing demand with
2 more NEW Presents every month—a total
of 8 NEW Harlequin Presents every month!

MORE of the most popular
romance fiction in the world!

*No one touches the heart of a woman
quite like Harlequin.*